SECOND DRAFT

C.M. SEABROOK

cm
SEABROOK

"It's much easier to become a father than to be one."

— KENT NERBURN

CHAPTER 1

LAYLA

I don't see the car, only hear the screech of tires, the horn blaring right before I'm being tossed to the ground, a large, very muscular body rolling with me.

Gravel bites into my skin, and the book I was reading flies from my grip.

The world flips a few times, and then stills.

A large hand cups the back of my head protectively, and an even larger body presses heavily between my thighs.

Above me, the sun shines behind the man's head, and it takes a few seconds for my eyes to adjust. But when they do, my breath catches in my throat.

Dark scruff shadows his face, but it only amplifies the sharp edges of his jaw, the small, sexy scar through his left eyebrow, the slight cleft in his chin, and the soft full lips that are parted slightly. But it's his eyes, the lightest shade of blue, seeming to radiate with an almost hypnotizing spark, that ignite something inside of me, and send little shockwaves of desire through every nerve ending in my body.

Maybe it's the adrenaline rush of almost dying, or the fact that it's been forever since I've had a man between my legs, but a tingle—or rather, an explosion of heat—that I haven't felt in years, races through my core, all the way down to my toes.

My hero stares down at me, his blue eyes dark, intense, and looking at me like he doesn't know whether to chastise me or kiss me.

Kiss me. The thought pops into my head, and I quickly suppress it. *Bad idea.*

My heart is pounding in my ears, and I know if I don't get this hulking giant off me soon, I'm going to do something even stupider than walking straight into mid-day traffic.

I push on his chest and wiggle beneath him, but that only makes the ache worse, because I can feel the enormous erection he's sporting, digging into my most intimate parts.

A small moan bubbles up inside my throat, and I have to clench my teeth to hold it back.

I swear the guy chuckles. I don't hear it, but I can feel it rumbling through his chest, and even though he may have just saved my life, I could slap him for it.

With slow, deliberate movements, he pushes himself up and away from me.

Damn, I wish he'd stayed there for just a few seconds longer.

Bad thoughts equal bad consequences, my mother's voice reprimands me.

And isn't that the truth. No one knows better than I do how quickly a good thing can turn into a disaster. It's one of the reasons I've sworn off sex, relationships – and men.

"You okay?" His voice is deep and resonates through my entire body.

I nod, unable to speak. Not because of my almost near-death experience, but because the guy crouching in front of me may just be the most gorgeous, sexy, *dangerous* man I've ever met.

Dressed in designer jeans that hang low on his narrow waist, and a tight black t-shirt that fits snug against his broad shoulders and chest, exposing the ink on both arms, he's got that dark, smoldering, I'll-eat-you-for-breakfast look.

And I have no doubt he would.

He's the epitome of everything my mother ever warned me about.

But despite my current vow of celibacy, even I'm not completely immune to a man who practically reeks of sex, especially one who just happened to swoop in and literally knock me off my feet while saving my life.

Yeah, I'm in trouble. *Big time.*

"Can you sit up?" One dark eyebrow is cocked, his gaze never leaving mine.

"I think so."

Wordlessly, he helps me to a sitting position, and his large, inked hands never leave my body. He tilts his chin, studying me, causing his almost black hair to flop to one side. Hair that's long on top and shaved on both sides, which only accentuates the bad boy vibe he's got going on.

There's a group of spectators watching us now, including a nervous-looking man who gets out of the rusty silver Toyota that almost hit me.

"Is she okay?" The little man strings his hands together, sweat beading on his brow.

"She's fine," my hero answers for me, then practically growls at the crowd. "Move on. There's nothing to see."

The command has people scattering, carrying on with their day as if they hadn't just witnessed a twenty-one-year-old woman walk directly into oncoming traffic because she was nose deep in chapter twenty-two of Vi Keeland's newest book. A book that now lays scattered across Main Street.

Damn it. I was only halfway through it, too.

"What the hell were you thinking?" My inked savior is staring at me, all dark and broody, like it was my plan to almost be run down. "You could have been killed."

I wince, knowing he's right, but I barely get any time to read. Not with juggling two jobs and trying to get my GED certificate at night.

He grunts, still watching me with a heaviness that makes my skin warm and my insides knot.

Unsteadily, I stand and dust off the pieces of gravel that stick to my jeans. "Thanks for pulling me back."

His mouth quirks up into the first semblance of a smile he's given me. But I'm not fooled. I know what's coming. I can see it in his eyes, in the way his body leans closer to me, drawing me to him like a magnet.

The guy has danger written all over him. Yeah, I wouldn't doubt it's written in ink somewhere on that beautiful, sculpted body.

His blue eyes twinkle, despite the intensity in his gaze. Slow and predator-like, he closes the distance between us, and I can feel the heat he produces like a flame on my skin.

"I can think of a way you can make it up to me." His tone is both playful and dripping with promise, and I can't help the shiver of anticipation that races down my spine.

"I'm sure you can," I mumble sarcastically, even though my body is begging to find out just how many ways I *can* make it up to him.

"Have dinner with me." The slant of his mouth, and the look in his eyes, is so self-assured, so confident, it's clear that he isn't used to being turned down.

"Just dinner?" I raise an eyebrow, knowing there's always a catch. A man like him would never want *just* dinner.

4

He pins me with a full-out smile, one that shows off the dimple in his cheek and leaves my knees turning to jelly. "Unless you'd like breakfast, too."

There it is. If I wasn't so damn hot and bothered right now, I'd probably chuckle at the predictability.

He leans in closer, his smile confident, almost arrogant, as if he's used to getting whatever he wants with just a single request.

To be honest, if I was any other person, one who wasn't completely terrified of what a man like him could do to a woman like me, I'd probably take him up on his offer.

"Thanks again for helping me." I start to turn, but he reaches for my wrist, and a thousand bolts of electricity race through my veins, sending a stabbing heat straight to my core.

Damn him. And damn the way my body responds. All warm and tingly, and willing at any second to throw itself into his arms.

His thumb strokes my skin, and his eyes search mine. His touch is like a Taser, making it impossible to move, or even speak.

"At least give me your name." His tone, dark and deep, skates over me like a rugged caress.

My mouth parts, and it takes me a few seconds to find my voice. "Layla."

"Layla." My name rolls off his tongue, and his gaze is filled with wicked intent.

Another shiver races down my spine, and I swear he knows it because his grin only broadens.

This man would destroy me. The small, unbroken fragments that are left of my heart wouldn't stand a chance against him.

Electricity.

Fire.

Those things can destroy. I've already been burned once, and I wasn't about to let it happen again.

"I have to go." Breaking the contact, I turn, and despite how ridiculous it seems – I run.

CHAPTER 2

CARTER

*T*he crowded bar throbs with house music, pulsating through me like the high I'm looking for. I need something, *anything* to dull the constant ache that presses between my ribs.

The past four years have been a goddamn avalanche of heartbreak. Tonight, I just want to drown my pain with booze and maybe a nice pair of tits. Because tomorrow, I hop on a plane to New York to start my new life as a sports journalist.

What a fucking joke.

The pay is shit. So is the magazine. But I'm not doing it for the money. That's not why I took the damn job. I took it because it's my only way to stay connected to my old life.

Hockey.

It's the only thing I cared about for years. Until fate decided to screw with, not only my family, but my career, too. Now that it's gone, it's like there's a piece of me missing.

An emptiness I can't seem to fill. It's stupid, I know. It's only a goddamn sport. But it's what defined me for so long that sometimes I don't really know who I am without it.

I snap open my prescription bottle and pop my last OxyContin, chasing it back with beer.

A shattered kneecap after being checked into the boards last spring ended my career in the NHL. Two surgeries and ten months of rehab later, my leg is still a mess. Chronic pain and sideline view of the game are all I have to look forward to now.

People are dancing and grinding as the lights flash and pulse to the rhythmic beat that thumps through the speakers.

It's not my typical scene, but seeing as it's my last night in town, I let my brother drag me here. Right now, though, I need a small break from Travis, who's currently doing Jager-bombs on the far side of the room with some chick he picked up twenty minutes after we got here.

At twenty-one, the kid—if I can still call him that—is living every teenaged boys' dream – on my paycheck. Unemployed, living off the money I give him each month, screwing countless women in the house I bought for him. Travis' only responsibility is not getting himself arrested – *again* – for disorderly conduct.

Sometimes, the seven years that separate us feel more like twenty. But then, I was never as set on self-destruction as Travis is.

That's not to say I haven't done my share of drinking and screwing hot women, but in everything I do, there's order and control.

Like now. My gaze scans the crowd, seeking the woman I'll take home tonight. Blonde, brunette, redhead; I don't care as long as she knows the rules – no strings attached. One night of pleasure. No phone numbers exchanged. Just sex.

Because it's all I have room for right now.

Not that I plan to stay single for the rest of my life. One day, I'll settle down and have a couple of kids, but that reality is so far from where I am right now that there's no sense pretending I want anything more than a good screw.

Sitting down at the bar, I order another Heineken and grin at the blonde on the stool next to me. She gives me the eyes—the ones that say "Fuck me please,"—and she leans closer, practically shoving her ample cleavage in my face.

"Hi." She bats her fake eyelashes at me. "Want to buy me a drink?"

It's almost too easy. I like a bit of a challenge. And the way I'm reading her, it would only take a few flattering words to have her blowing me in the basement restroom.

Not what I'm looking for tonight.

I grunt and shake my head, causing her to pout, then turn back to the guy she was previously hitting on.

Paying for my beer, I'm about to walk away when my gaze lands on a figure sitting in the shadows at the far end of the bar. *Layla.* The girl who'd practically ran from me after I'd saved her life. The girl I hadn't been able to get out of my head for the past two weeks.

Light brown hair hangs in waves over her shoulders, and her brows turn down intently as her gaze skims the pages of the book she's reading. She's fucking reading, *in a bar.* I almost chuckle at how out of place she looks, until she glances up and meets my gaze with those eyes.

It's not just the color, which in this light looks like a soft brown, the color of caramel – it's what's beneath them.

Innocence.

Warmth.

The complete opposite of everything I am.

Those eyes go wide with recognition when they land on me, and I see it, the spark of lust she hadn't been able to hide, despite her attempt.

I give her one of my crooked smiles, the one that usually has women begging me to fuck them. Her cheeks turn red, and she quickly looks back down at the book in her hand.

A small chuckle rumbles in my throat, because no matter how hard she tries to hide it, I can see she's into me. I felt it in her body when I'd been on top of her. The heat. The need that radiated off her in waves.

But I know what she sees when she looks at me – *danger*.

It's not only that I'm big; at six foot four, I tower over most men. And it's not the ink that covers my arms in full sleeves. It's not even the muscles that bunch and coil with my every movement. It's the darkness I carry with me, like a black aura, pushing everyone away. Even my own damn brother.

She's right to be afraid, because in all fairness, she's too young for me. Too innocent for the things I want to do to her.

Hell, she barely looks old enough to be in this place.

And me? I may only be twenty-eight, but I'm as tainted as they come.

Broken?

No.

My wounds have healed, but not without leaving thick, impenetrable scars on my body and my soul.

I should walk away, but my cock won't let me. It's begging me to cross the fifteen feet of space between us and make her mine – at least for tonight.

I'm not the only guy who's noticed her.

With gritted teeth, I watch as a meathead-looking dude approaches her, a cocky ass grin on his ugly face. Across the room, a table of rowdy guys yell out a few crude comments, edging him forward.

He leans on the bar in front of her, getting in her personal space.

If it wasn't there before, it is now. The big fuck-off sign plastered on her forehead. But the guy either doesn't notice, or doesn't care.

Yeah, so not going to happen, buddy. I almost feel sorry for the bastard, until he puts his hands on her.

He reaches out and drags his fingers down her bare arm. It's a subtle touch, but it stirs the inner caveman inside of me.

Walk away, Carter, I tell myself. No girl is worth a fight. Especially not a bar fight.

But, hell, the overprotective Neanderthal part of my brain kicks into high gear, muting out all common sense.

The guy is practically mauling her by the time I cross the distance between us.

"Come and have a drink with us," he slurs, wrapping a meaty arm around her shoulders, leaning in heavily.

There's fear in her eyes when she places her hands on his chest, trying to push him away. "I'm waiting for–"

"Me," I growl out, my voice rumbling above the music.

The guy turns in my direction and gives me a look that says he doesn't believe me, then his eyes widen slightly in recognition.

Fuck. It doesn't happen very often anymore, but it's always uncomfortable when it does.

"Oh shit. You're–"

"Your worst enemy if you don't get your hands off my girl." I don't need him announcing to the whole bar who I am. Or more accurately, who I was.

Carter "The Crusher" Bennett. I was the New York Rangers second draft pick almost a decade ago, and I sent more guys home on a stretcher than any rookie that first year, also placing a giant target on my back while doing it.

"Sorry, man. I didn't realize." The guy stands abruptly, putting his hands in the air and taking a couple of steps back. But he's still watching me, and so is Layla.

"Hey, sweetheart. Sorry I'm late." I place an arm possessively around her shoulders.

"You're right on time." She gives me a look that says she doesn't know if I've just saved her, or put her in more danger.

More danger, sweetheart. Much more.

I watch her doe-like gaze as I lean in and press my lips against hers.

Her hands come up to my chest, but she doesn't push me away. Instead, she leans into the kiss, and I feel her body tremble against mine.

Like I expected, the chemistry between us is off-the-charts intense.

Deep inside of me, something stirs, and something foreign shivers through my senses.

Damn, the woman does something to me. Something I haven't felt before.

Hating to break the contact, but knowing the douchebag is still watching us, I slowly pull back, my gaze locked on hers.

"You mind?" I raise an eyebrow at the guy who's looking at me like I'm a celebrity or something.

Which I'm not.

At least, not anymore.

He turns back to his buddies, and I hear my name being tossed around amongst them.

"You okay?" I lean against the bar and see her gaze linger across the ink on my forearm, following the pattern until it disappears beneath my t-shirt.

Her lips tighten and she swallows hard. "You didn't have to kiss me," she says, trying her best to feign indignation, but her gaze rests on my mouth, and I can practically feel her body begging me for more.

"No." I grin, trying to suppress the small chuckle that rises in my throat. "But I wanted to."

She licks her lips, a mix of fear and excitement in her eyes. "Apparently, sitting alone means I'm looking for someone to take me home."

"Are you?"

"No." She shakes her head, but again her gaze trails down my torso.

"You sure about that?" I raise an eyebrow, smirking.

Immediately, her cheeks turn scarlet and she looks away. "I'm just waiting for my roommate. She works here and I'm picking her up..." She lets out a small, frustrated breath. "I don't know why I'm explaining myself to you."

She's definitely got the good girl act down. If it *is* an act. She's pretty convincing. I stay away from her type, because I know they always expect more. She's not the kind of girl that just hooks up for a night. And that's all I'm looking for.

But my mind races with all the things I want to do to her. My body aches with the need to taste her again, to hear my name on her lips when I drive myself balls-deep inside of her.

You'll only break her, my brain warns. There's something fragile about her, something that makes me want to do more than just fuck her. An unfamiliar need to both possess and protect her.

I know I should walk away, leave her to her book. But she has me intrigued, wanting to know more about her.

"Can I buy you a drink while you're waiting for your friend?"

"I'm good with water."

I chuckle.

"What?" Her eyes narrow.

"You're an enigma."

"An enigma?" She frowns.

"A mystery, a puzzle. Something difficult to understand."

"I know what the word means." There's a hint of frustration in her voice. "I just meant, *how?*"

"You're reading a book in a bar. You kind of stand out."

She glances down at the novel and shrugs.

"It also doesn't hurt that you look like a…"

Her head jerks up, her gaze hard on me like I was about to insult her, which is the furthest thing from the truth.

"Like a what?" she demands.

"Nothing."

"No. Say it. Like a what?"

Like a good girl that's just begging for a real man to fuck the innocence out of her.

"Like a librarian."

"A librarian?" She glances down at the white button-down shirt and black skirt she's wearing and frowns.

"Or a school girl. But not one of the naughty ones–"

"Okay, I get it." She rolls her eyes. "I just came from work."

"At the library?" I laugh, teasing.

"No." She tucks her hair behind her ear nervously, and admits with a small smile, "A bookstore."

Of course. That's the first thing about the girl that's made sense to me.

Without thinking, I reach out and trace the curve of her jaw, and I feel her tremble beneath my touch.

Her eyes widen as she sucks in a shuddering breath, her expression churning with uncertainty and confusion. Desire. Need. Fear.

Everything about the girl screams innocence.

I pull my hand back, and she lets out the breath she was holding.

"Are you even old enough to be in here?"

"I'm twenty-one." Her chin juts out defensively.

The same age as Travis. And yet, they couldn't be more different. There's a vulnerability to her, but also a strength.

I lean back, my elbows resting on the bar. "So, you're twenty-one. You like to read...in a bar, on a Saturday night, while drinking water–"

"I told you, I'm waiting for my friend."

Friend. Not a boyfriend.

"What else do you do?"

"Why?"

"You intrigue me. And I want to know more about you."

Her brows are tightly drawn down and she's watching me like she can't figure out the game I'm playing. But the truth is, it isn't a game. I'm genuinely interested to know what makes her tick.

She glances down at the book in her hand, suddenly looking extremely vulnerable. "I write."

"Really?"

"I wrote a book." Her cheeks flame at the admission.

"Impressive."

"Not really. It never got published." Her tongue darts out across her soft, pink lips, and I can't help the filthy thoughts that fill my mind—her on her knees in front of me, lips stretched around my cock.

Holy hell, when was the last time I'd had this reaction to a woman? Maybe never.

I clear my throat. "What's it about? The book."

A small grin plays on her lips. "Oh, you know, the whole good girl meets the bad boy in a bar, they fall in love instantly, and live happily ever after."

I pause, something stirring in my chest.

"Really?"

She laughs and shakes her head. "No. I'm kidding. But *that* would probably get published. Because that's what people want."

"Bad boys?"

"Yeah." She nods. "And happily ever afters."

"Ah, the stuff of fairytales." I take a swig of my beer.

"Exactly."

"So, write that story."

She shrugs. "I can't write what I don't believe."

Interesting.

"You don't believe in happy endings?"

She shrugs. "Life is just so much messier. Think about it. How many people do you know who are living their dream? Or, who've found *the one?*"

I open my mouth, then shut it, because she's right. I can't think of one. Except maybe my parents. They had the marriage books are written about, but then...bam. One drunk driver, and both of their lives were snuffed out too soon.

My chest tightens at the memory. Four years has done little to dull the pain.

"Maybe that's why people want to read that stuff."

"Why?"

"A way to forget the shittiness of life. To believe in something that will fill the gaping wound in their chests."

"You're probably right." She tilts her head, studying me, like she can see right to my core.

It's unnerving, and yet so fucking tempting. To remove the detachment I usually carry around with me like a shield, and let her see the darkest, most tainted parts of me. Maybe it's because I see it in her, too. Secrets and demons that haunt those beautiful eyes.

"And you?" She asks, gaze boring into mine with an intimacy that makes my heart race. "Is that what you're looking for? To fill the gaping wound in your chest?"

"I don't read romance novels." I grin, until I realize how close to the truth it actually is. Instead of books, I just use alcohol and pills to push through the haze of regret and loss.

"Layla, you ready?" A strawberry blonde stands at the edge of the bar, watching us, brows raised.

"Coming." Layla slides off the stool and gives me a small smile, then starts towards her friend.

Am I really going to let her walk away? It's been years since I've felt anything but grief, but this woman stirs something inside of me.

Hope.

A desire to change.

A desire for more than just unbridled sex with nameless women.

"Layla," I growl out her name, watching her body react in a way that makes my cock harden painfully.

She turns, drawing her bottom lip between her teeth, brows raised. "Yes?"

I grab a pen that's sitting in a cup on the bar, then scribble my number on one of the paper coasters.

"Here." I hand it to her. "I'm going out of town for a few months, but when I get back, I'd love to read your book. I know a really good publicist, and I'm sure I could get him to look at it."

She blushes. "Like I said, it's not very good. The ending–"

"Can always be altered." I lean down, my mouth close to her ear. "And maybe I can change your mind."

She looks at me with confusion. "About what?"

"Happy endings." I cup her chin and tilt her face up, then lean in so that our lips are almost touching. "Finding *the one*."

Because, as crazy as it seems, part of me wonders if I've just found mine. I've never believed in love at first sight, or fairytales, but I'm pretty sure this woman is a whole lot of everything that I need.

Her breath hitches, and her eyes widen.

17

"Layla, come on. Max is waiting," her friend complains, popping her gum and texting frantically on her phone.

She gives me an apologetic smile. "I really have to go–"

I crush my lips against hers. This time, there's nothing soft or innocent about the kiss. It's hard, demanding, a promise of what I want to give her.

On a breathy sigh, her lips part, and she melts against me.

Pure, undiluted pleasure.

When I pull back, I grin down at her. "Call me."

She nods, eyes glazed and face flushed, then turns and walks away, glancing over her shoulder before disappearing into the crowd.

I drag my fingers through my hair and let out a heavy breath, hating that I'm just letting her go. Even though she has my number, there's no guarantee that she'll call.

My number...

Shit. I realize my screw up. I'd changed servers a few days ago for my new job, and I'm pretty sure I gave her my old cell number.

Normally, I wouldn't care. It's not like I don't have a lineup of women begging to jump in my bed. But the thought of not seeing her again makes my stomach clench.

I move through the bar quickly and push open the metal door, shivering when a cool blast of air hits me.

The parking lot is packed with people, but none of them are Layla.

Damn it. I comb my fingers over my face and curse.

She's gone. And I have no idea if I'll ever see her again.

CHAPTER 3

CARTER

One Year Later...

A line of cars outside my house is my first indication that my brother is throwing a party. The second is the thumping music that vibrates through the bay windows. *Fuck.*

I was hoping to get Travis alone.

He wouldn't tell me over the phone, but I'm pretty sure he's dug himself into another hole. One that I'm going to have to bail him out of – again.

This shit is getting old. And so am I. Too old to be cleaning up after him.

Sure, I've done things I'm not proud of, but there comes a time when you need to grow the hell up.

From the foyer, I can see a handful of people in the living room, and another half dozen in the kitchen. But no sign of my brother anywhere.

I drop my luggage at the front door, and a few heads turn to look in my direction, then continue on with whatever they'd been doing, which consists mostly of drinking and smoking up.

The house smells like a goddamn fraternity. Beer. Cigarettes. Pot. Sex.

There's a group of three guys sharing a bong on the living room couch. A couch I just replaced six months ago because Travis' buddies set fire to the old one, nearly burning down the damn house.

"Do you know where Travis is?" I growl out.

One of them looks up, eyes glazed. "He's with some chick upstairs."

I shake my head when he raises the bong for me to take.

This shit has got to stop.

I take the stairs and pound on Travis' door.

"Busy," is the muffled reply, followed by a woman's moan.

"Travis, open the fucking door."

There are a few curses followed by a couple thumps before the door opens, and my brother stands half naked in front of me.

"Nice party," I say sarcastically, getting a full glimpse of the redhead's breasts before she pulls her top over her head.

Her eyes rake over me and she gives me an appreciative smile.

Ignoring her, I glance back at Travis, who takes the t-shirt the woman hands him and shrugs it on.

He motions for the girl to leave with a dismissive tilt of his head.

"I didn't expect you until next week," he says, dragging his fingers through his shaggy, brown hair.

"Obviously."

He grabs a half empty beer bottle off his desk and chugs it back, then looks at me and slurs, "What're you doing here?"

Technically, it's my house. I don't need a reason. But I've let him live here so long that I swear he forgets who pays the bills.

"Your text sounded pretty urgent."

He shrugs, but I see the guilt that crosses his expression. "I'm just dealing with a lot of shit right now."

From the way he shifts to lean against the wall, I'm thinking he's got a good six or seven beers in him.

"You're not in jail, so I assume it's about money."

"Ouch." He winces, rubbing the back of his neck.

"How much?"

"Want a drink? I'll grab you one–"

"How much, Travis?" I hate being an ass, but I need to know the damage. I do well enough, but the last time I received a text like the one I got the other night, it ended up costing me forty grand in property damage and another five in lawyers' fees.

"It's not about money." Travis sucks his top lip over his teeth and looks away.

Shit. This is going to be bad.

"What is it then?" My stomach twists.

"You just got here. We can talk about it tomorrow."

"Tomorrow?" So it isn't that urgent. The squeezing in my chest subsides slightly, but in the back of my head there's a flashing neon sign warning me it's not going to be a simple fix this time. "Fine."

I'm already in a pissy mood after an hour's delay on my flight. And my knee is throbbing from sitting for so long. I'll probably handle whatever he has to say better after a good night's sleep.

I start down the stairs towards the kitchen and say over my shoulder, "You mind telling your buddies to take the party somewhere else?"

"Seriously, bro?" Travis' hands slam down on my shoulders. "Come on, have a couple beers with us. When's the last time the two of us got tanked together?" He gives me one of his easygoing grins. "Or better yet, stoned?"

"One beer."

"Good man."

I grunt, following him into the crowded kitchen, choking on the fumes.

"I'll meet you in the back. I need some fresh air."

Travis nods before being dragged into a conversation with a guy sucking back a joint.

I head through the sliding doors that lead to the back-yard, breathing in the fresh air.

Boxes of empty beer bottles line the back of the house, but other than that, it looks like Travis has actually kept the yard up. There are even flowers in the few pots that sit on the large wooden deck.

I frown at that, because I know there's no way in hell that Travis planted any damn flowers.

Maybe they're just weeds. I pick one of them, and look at it more closely.

"Definitely not a weed," I mutter.

"They're begonias," a woman says behind me.

I glance over my shoulder, following the sound of the voice, and freeze.

All I see are her eyes. Those soft brown eyes that could pierce a man's heart, and make him wish he were a better man.

I'd know them anywhere.

Layla.

Sitting on the old wooden swing, with another damn book in her hands, she blinks up at me, eyes wide. "You?"

I can't believe my luck. I doubted I'd ever see her again when she walked out of that bar.

"What are you doing here?" It's a stupid question. The

answer is obvious. She's friends with Travis somehow. The thought makes my stomach tighten.

"I–" Her face turns a shade of red, clearly as flustered by my presence as I am by hers. She shuts her book and stands. A small frown tugs at her lips. "I live here."

"Here?" I blink in confusion.

Travis said he was getting a roommate, someone to help pay the bills. Which is ridiculous, because I already pay them. But I couldn't fault him for being resourceful.

"Yeah." She continues to frown up at me.

"You live here, in my house?" I laugh, because what are the fucking odds?

"Your house?" Her face pales. "Oh my God. You're Travis' brother?"

There's something in the way she says it that makes me uneasy. A premonition that leaves my heart thudding painfully in my chest.

"He is." Travis comes through the sliding doors carrying two beers. He hands me one, then slaps me on the back, hard enough that it makes me grunt. "My big, perfect brother. Saint fucking Carter."

"Don't be an ass." I give him a look of warning, but he's either too drunk to notice or he doesn't care.

"But it's my thing." Travis grabs Layla around the waist and plants a hard kiss on her cheek. "It's what the girls love about me. Right, darling?"

"You're drunk." She squirms in his arms, trying to get away.

"Not yet. But I plan to be real soon." He takes a deep swallow of the beer he's holding, then releases her.

I can't figure out the dynamics between them, but I know instantly that something is up. The tension is practically tangible.

Is she sleeping with him? From the little I know about her, I wouldn't have thought she'd go for someone like Travis. But then, I really *don't* know anything about her. Just that she's obsessed with reading – and she's living in my house.

Layla's gaze flickers to mine, clearly uncomfortable.

Someone shouts at Travis from the house.

"I'll be right back." He hits me again on the shoulder, and I swear I'm going to put him in a goddamn headlock the next time he touches me. "Make yourself at home."

Is he fucking serious?

God, the kid has it coming to him.

An awkward silence stretches between us before I finally ask, "So, you and Travis?"

"No." She shakes her head, and her cheeks redden before she looks away. "It's complicated."

Complicated.

Shit. I know what that means.

Remembering the girl Travis was probably screwing upstairs, I'd say complicated was an understatement.

Best case scenario, she has a crush on him. Worst, she's sleeping with him. But there's no doubt in my mind that they are involved somehow.

I want to ask, to dig deeper, but there's also a part of me that doesn't want to know.

"How long have you been living here?" I take a deep sip of my beer, watching her.

"A few months. Travis lets me stay for practically nothing as long as I cook and clean." She fidgets with the book in her hand. "I didn't know you and him were...I would never have…"

"You don't have to explain."

Her cheeks are still red. "Are you staying here?"

"I was planning on it, but if it's going to be awkward I can go to a hotel."

She shakes her head. "This is your place. If you want me to leave–"

"No," I say a little too quickly. "It's fine."

I just fucking found her again, so the last thing I want is for her to disappear. A year of fantasies, a need I couldn't shake. I obsessed about her, wanting to possess every sweet innocent inch of her perfect body. Consume her until there wasn't anything left.

I still do.

But if she really is with Travis, I may just be torturing myself by sticking around.

I scrub a hand over my face, feeling the hair scrape against my palm.

She pulls her bottom lip into her mouth and looks at anything but me. I wonder if I should mention the wrong cell number, but then if she hadn't tried calling, it'll just make me look like a jackass.

"I'm going to turn in for the night," she says awkwardly, pointing with her thumb at the house.

Say something, asshole.

"It's good to see you again."

She gives a small smile that doesn't reach her eyes.

"Layla?"

She stops at the sliding doors and glances over her shoulder. "Yeah?"

"I meant what I said. I do want to read your book." I hadn't lied about that. In fact, it was one of the things I hadn't stopped thinking about. Which is fucking weird, because I don't even like reading.

A small frown twists her lips and she shakes her head. "I've given up on that. Writing just isn't my thing."

I want to call bullshit, but she disappears before I get the chance. The thought of following her crosses my mind. But if she's with Travis, in any way, I need to stay as far away from her as possible.

I finish the last of my beer, then head inside.

Travis is in the living room with his bong-buddies, smoking the thing back like it's oxygen.

As much as I want to right now, I can't leave. I still have to deal with whatever shit he's got himself into.

Picking up my bags, I tramp up the stairs towards my old room. Travis' door is open, and a quick glance lets me know that Layla isn't in there. That's one positive.

The third bedroom at the end of the hall is closed, and there's a soft light underneath the door.

At least I know she has her own room. Not that it's much of a comfort. Because the more I think about it, the more I realize that complicated can only mean one thing – sex.

I've never been jealous of my brother. Not until right now.

I toss my bags in the corner of my room, then shut the door.

She was supposed to be mine. The thought comes unbidden, from a primal part of my brain. The part that's beating its chest right now, demanding that I claim her, fill her with my cock, and make her scream my name so loudly she'll forget all others.

Swiping a hand over my face, then through my hair, I let out a heavy sigh. I'm used to life throwing curve balls, but this is one I didn't see coming.

CHAPTER 4

LAYLA

*T*ravis glares at me over his coffee cup, leaning against the kitchen counter. He's obviously sporting a wicked hangover. His eyes are rimmed red, and his hair is sticking up in all different directions. The girl who was in his bed last night left a few minutes ago, and now his full attention is on me. I can see him stewing for another fight.

Not today, please, I want to beg. Not when his brother, the man I've been dreaming about for the past year, is sleeping right above us.

"You've got to get rid of it." Travis' words are casual, like he's talking about an old sweater, or piece of furniture that he wants taken to the dump, and not an actual human being.

"I can't." We've had this argument multiple times since I told him I was pregnant. And every time, it ends with him storming out of the house, and me in tears. Not because I really care what Travis thinks, but because I have no idea how I'm going to raise this baby on my own.

"It's not even a baby yet," he sneers, dragging his fingers through his brown hair. "It's just a mass of cells. I don't get what your problem is."

I can't explain the way I feel, not to him. Even if I did, I know he'd never understand.

"You're being so fucking selfish." He slams his cup on the counter, his voice getting louder. "This is *my* life, too."

"I told you. I don't want anything from you."

"Bullshit." He grabs the bottle of vodka off the counter and pours some into his coffee.

It's not even nine in the morning and he's already drinking. But that's what he does. Drinks. Parties. Sleeps with countless women. It was a mistake to move in with him. Our lives are so completely different. But then, I've made a lot of mistakes in the last few months as well. Mistakes I promised I would never make again.

I need to get out of here, and not just for the moment. I need to find a new place to live, as soon as possible.

"I'll move out as soon as–"

"So, then I'm the asshole who kicked his pregnant girl-friend out of the house?"

"I'm not your girlfriend." I never was. It was just sex between us, and only once.

I'd been drinking – my first mistake. I don't drink, or I usually don't. But I'd had a really shitty week. I'd only meant to have one, maybe two beers. But then Travis' friends came over, and they kept offering me drinks.

By the time I'd stumbled to my room and stripped off my clothes, I was plastered. When Travis crawled in beside me, I didn't push him away – my second mistake.

Travis swears he used protection, but I can't remember if

he did or not. Either way, he got me knocked up. I'm just glad I didn't get something worse, like an STD.

"Fuck, Layla." He begins to pace. "I'm not ready to be a father."

"I'm not asking you to be."

"If you're keeping it, you are."

"I didn't want this either, but–"

"I'm starting to wonder if maybe you did."

"Excuse me?" Is he kidding? I've never been a violent person, but right now I'm ready to slap him. My fingers wrap around the back of the kitchen chair, my knuckles whitening. "You'd better not be saying I planned this."

"It just seems odd. We only slept together one fucking time, and it wasn't even that good–"

"You really are an asshole."

"And you're being a selfish bitch." Travis' eyes burn with a mix of anger and fear. "If you think you're going to trap me into marrying you, think again."

"I didn't even *want* to sleep with you. And I wouldn't have if I hadn't been drunk."

"You didn't say no."

"Because I was practically passed out."

Travis' face is bright red, but I can see the guilt there. Because he knows it's the truth.

"Everything okay in here?" Carter stands in the doorway, looking between us, a dark scowl marring his handsome features.

He's wearing low-rise jeans and a dark t-shirt that does little to hide the corded muscles and broad shoulders beneath. Dark hair hangs in damp waves over his forehead, but it's his blue and piercing eyes that hold me.

"Everything's just peachy," Travis says derisively, crossing his arms over his chest and looking out the window.

"Layla?" Carter asks me.

"Fine," I mumble. *Had he heard what we'd been talking about?*

I know he'll find out eventually, but I prefer not to be around when he does.

What terrible luck, that the man I've been fantasizing about for the past year is the brother of the man I'm ready to strangle right now. The man whose baby I'm having.

Carter moves around the table, grabbing a coffee cup from the cupboards. "I'm going to get a room at the Radisson and stay there until I figure out where I'm going next."

"Why?" Travis' brows draw down as he scowls.

Side by side, I can see the resemblance.

Carter's hair is darker, his eyes a lighter shade of blue, and his body covered in a beautiful, twisted pattern of ink. But they have the same bone structure, the same lush bottom lip, and the same sullen broodiness that makes them both insufferably sexy, and incredible dangerous.

"I just think it's better that way." Carter watches me over his coffee cup as he takes his first sip.

"Whatever." Travis glowers at him, then tosses his mug in the sink. "You can do whatever the hell you want to do. You always do."

"Someone woke up in a shitty mood." Carter leans against the counter, one ankle crossed over the other, his biceps bulging when he lifts his cup to his lips.

"Screw off." The tension radiating off Travis is almost violent. "Both of you."

I've got to get out of here before I say something I shouldn't. Or worse, start to cry.

"Where are you going?" Travis glares at me when I grab my purse off the table.

"Some of us have to work," I snap.

He grabs my arm when I walk past him. "We're not finished talking."

I peel his fingers back. "Yes, we are."

Ignoring Carter's watchful gaze, I slip out of the kitchen and make a beeline for the front door. Angry words follow me out, but this time it's Carter yelling at Travis. I can't hear exactly what he says, but I can tell he isn't happy.

I almost make it to my car when I hear the front door open behind me.

"Layla. Stop." Carter's voice is deep and commanding, like liquid heat stroking my skin and making my insides turn to molten lava.

I turn, my gaze lifting over his powerful chest, up his inked throat to his handsome face.

Damn, why does he have to be so freaking hot?

His dark brows are drawn down, his blue eyes full of concern.

I can't do this right now. My hands are already shaking, and tears blur my vision. I still can't believe that he's Travis' brother. I swear, fate has it in for me.

I've spent almost a year dreaming about those eyes, and the taste of his lips on mine.

I've never been kissed like that. *Ever.*

I'd been on a high for days afterwards, debating whether or not to call him. A week later, I finally built up the nerve to dial the number. But his damn phone had either been disconnected, or worse, he'd given me fake digits.

In a way, I believed it was for the best. I didn't expect to see him again. But here he is, standing in front of me, all sexy and brooding – and he's the brother of the man whose baby I'm carrying.

Fucking perfect.

"Are you all right?" He tilts his head, studying me.

"I'm running late." I fidget with my keys, and look down at my hands.

"What's going on?"

My back teeth grind together, and I look away. "You should ask Travis."

"I'm asking you." He leans in, so close I can smell his scent, and I feel his warm breath on my cheek.

"It's...complicated."

"Yeah." He rubs the back of his neck. "You said that last night."

"Look. I don't want to get in the middle of you and Travis. You're his family, and I'm..." I swallow hard and look away again. "I'm just some girl that got mixed up with the wrong guy."

Or more specifically, the wrong brother.

Carter's nostrils flare and he glances back at the house, his eyes narrowed, like he's ready to beat the shit out of his brother. "I don't know what he did—"

"He didn't do anything." That's not technically true, but it isn't my place to tell him what happened. God, this is awkward. "You really need to talk to Travis. I know you two aren't that close, but—"

"He told you that?"

I shrug. "It's kind of obvious. But you're still brothers. And this whole situation is just going to get more difficult once..."

Shit.

"Once what?" he demands.

Once I have your brother's baby.

"Just give me a couple days to get my stuff together and I'll be out of here." I open the driver's side door, then get in.

Carter shoves his hands in the pockets of his jeans, but he doesn't move, even as I start to pull out of the driveway.

Once I turn the corner, far from his prying gaze, I let out the shaky breath I was holding in. With trembling fingers, I pull out my cell and dial Kira.

"Bar guy is back," I say when she answers, trying desperately to suppress the emotions stirring in my chest.

"Really? You saw him?" Of all the people in this messed-up world, Kira knows me the best. She also knows what that night in the bar did to me. For a few short days, it made me believe again. Believe that life isn't always so cruel, and that maybe there really are happy endings, even for girls like me.

Such bullshit.

"So?" Kira pushes.

"He's Travis' brother." There it is. The big cosmic joke. I swear, if there is a God, he's somewhere up there having a good laugh at my expense. Or maybe this is my punishment for being the little slut my mom always accused me of being.

There's a long stretch of silence before Kira responds. "Oh, shit."

Oh, shit is right.

"What are you going to do?"

"Nothing. Except move out."

"But–"

"I can't stay there any longer. Especially not when Carter is there, too."

"Carter?"

"Bar guy."

"Right." There's a heavy breath on the other end. "You know I'd let you stay with us if there was room."

"I know." Kira moved into a bachelor apartment four months ago with her current boyfriend, Max. It's the reason I had to find a new place, because I couldn't afford the rent at the old one without her.

I'm happy for her, though. The two of them are cute together, and the guy seems to genuinely care about her, which is something.

It was Max who introduced me to Travis and suggested I move in with him. Travis was looking more for a maid than a roommate, but the rent was cheap, and it was the first time I'd actually lived in a house and not some rundown apartment since I'd run away from home seven years before.

Everything was good at first. Travis was easy to get along with, if I ignored his excessive drinking, smoking, and the rotating string of women he brought home.

I liked having a backyard to plant flowers, and a large kitchen to make meals. And to cook for someone who actually enjoyed the different recipes I tried.

Kira had always been so picky, preferring macaroni and cheese over the fancier meals I made, like chicken parmesan or eggplant lasagna.

I'd been warned that Travis was a playboy, but I'd moved in on roommate-only terms. And I'd spent the last seven years running from temptation. I didn't have any worries where he was concerned, because I never intended for anything to happen between us.

Travis, being Travis, had other ideas.

Two weeks in to living with him, I knew I was in trouble. He was all over me. It started out as innocent flirting, but quickly escalated when he realized I wasn't falling for his typical moves.

It wasn't that I didn't find him attractive. Travis is gorgeous in that California surfer boy way. Dimples, rock hard body, and a carefree charm that makes you wish you could spend your day lounging in the sun.

But he wasn't my bar guy. He was the one who haunted my dreams with his intense blue gaze and soft, full lips.

The one.

At least, that's what my overdramatic brain believed.

And this is why little girls should never read fairytales. Because they're complete and utter rubbish.

"Layla?" Kira's voice breaks through my thoughts.

"Sorry. I was just thinking."

She sighs, but there's only sympathy when she says, "You're sure you want to go through with this?"

No. I'm not sure. I'm not sure about anything.

I blink back the tears that are blurring my vision. "I can't get rid of it."

"I know." And she does. She's one of the only people in this world that knows why I won't have an abortion. Why I'd never survive that. "I just meant that there are other options."

Adoption. It's something that crossed my mind. But the thought leaves a black hole burning in my chest.

"I'm twenty-two. Not fifteen. There's no reason I can't raise this baby on my own."

"You know I'm here for you no matter what you decide."

"I know. Thank you." I end the call as I pull into the parking lot of the animal shelter.

I've already made my decision. I know it isn't going to be easy, but the choice is mine to make. I'll sign whatever paperwork Travis wants me to sign to relieve him of all obligations. It's probably better that way.

I can do this.

Without Travis.

Without Carter.

It's that second thought that makes my throat tighten. Because I realize now that despite everything, up until the moment he told me he was Travis' brother, I actually believed that one day my bar guy, the guy who'd saved my life, my own dark hero, would walk into my life again and maybe – just maybe – I really would get my happy ending.

I swipe my tears away with the back of my hand and look in the mirror at the blotchy face that stares back at me.

Time to toughen up, because the reality is, there's no white knight coming to my rescue this time.

CHAPTER 5

CARTER

"She's pregnant?" I stare at my brother in disbelief. Jealousy wars with anger, and that fucking caveman inside me beats his chest in outrage.

Every possessive, territorial bone in my body wants it to be a lie, but looking at my brother's pathetic, guilty face, I know it's the truth.

"Yes." He paces the living room, and his fingers curl into fists at his sides.

He looks like he's ready to hit something.

In a way, I wouldn't mind if he took a swing at me. At least it would give me a reason to hit him back. Because right now, I really, *really* want to.

"And it's yours?" I growl out, my throat constricting over the words. I doubt Layla would lie about something like that, but I have to ask.

"If it was any other fucking girl, I'd wonder, but Layla doesn't sleep around. Shit, I practically had to force her to sleep with me. It was like trying to get Mother Teresa to spread her damn legs."

"Did you force her?" I take a step towards him, and there must be murder in my eyes because he quickly takes a step back, hands raised with his palms towards me.

"What the hell, Carter? It was a joke."

"Not a funny one." I narrow my gaze, not knowing what to believe from him right now.

The thought of him forcing himself on her makes me see red. He may be my brother, but I'm pretty sure I'd go to prison for the things I'd do to him if I ever found out that *that* was the case.

"The totally messed-up part about this whole thing is that I only fucked her once. Who gets pregnant after one lousy screw?"

I have to shove my hands in my pocket to keep myself from knocking the pitiful look off his face.

"I can't do this," Travis whines, sitting down on the couch and placing his head in his hands.

"Then you should have kept your dick in your pants. You're going to be a father. It's not like you have a choice."

"She said she's giving me one."

"What do you mean?" Something dark stirs inside of me.

"She's going to talk to a lawyer. I can waive my rights and–"

"You're not seriously considering it? Shit. This is your kid you're talking about."

"But it doesn't have to be," he says, like some damn paper will just erase the fact that the baby is his. "I'm twenty-two years old. I've barely started to live."

"So what? You're just going to pretend like this never happened? Walk around like there's not some kid out there wearing your face? Jesus, Travis. Mom and Dad would be so fucking proud."

He glares at me, then leans back on the couch and squeezes his eyes shut. "If she'd just get an abortion, everything would be fine."

"Is she considering it?" I don't know why, but the thought makes my chest tighten.

"No." He throws his hands in the air and stands again, starting to pace. "I don't get it. She's not even religious."

"You don't have to be religious to want to keep your child. To have a family."

"Here we go again. Saint fucking Carter on his moral high horse."

"Don't do that. We've both made mistakes."

"Yeah." He narrows his eyes on me. "*We* have."

I know where his mind is going. The same dark memory that haunts my dreams. The one choice he'll never forgive me for making.

"I'm just saying, this kid is your family."

"Since when have you cared so much about family?" Travis' lips curl up in a snarl, and there's something almost feral in his expression.

His words bite, because I know there's truth to them.

I haven't been around. Maybe if I had, things would have turned out differently. It was a shit thing to do, leaving him alone when he was only seventeen. No parents. No rules. No one to be accountable to.

But I had my career. And back then, hockey was everything to me. I wasn't about to give up my shot playing with the pros to come home and take care of a kid that was already practically grown.

"What do you want from me? An apology? I did what I had to do."

"You did what you had to do for yourself. Don't try and twist it any other way."

I stay silent, because he's right.

Travis pulls out a pack of smokes from his back pocket, and lights one.

"I'm just saying, we aren't that different. You were my age when Mom and Dad died. You didn't want to be settled down with a kid. I get it now."

"What I did was completely different. You were my brother, and you were seventeen."

Travis shrugs. "Maybe."

I shake my head at him. "So, what're your plans?"

"I don't know. I just know I have to get out of here. Maybe travel a bit." He butts the cigarette out in a dirty glass that sits on the fireplace mantle. "There's a job up north I'm looking into."

"What kind of job?" He hasn't been able to hold down a job for more than three months at a time. With the money from our parents' accident settlement, he's been able to live pretty comfortably without having to.

Until recently.

The way our parents had it worked out, he'd only received small chunks each month until he was twenty-one. After that, he had access to the whole lump sum, which he blasted through on God knows what over the past year.

"There's a construction site up in British Colombia–"

"Canada?"

"Yeah."

I want to punch the little bastard. "You're kidding me, right?"

"It's good money."

"And it would get you out of here," I say, knowing that's the main reason he's even considering it.

He nods slowly and looks out the large bay window, his blue eyes unreadable.

"And Layla? What do you plan to do about her?"

"I thought she could stay here. At least until she finds a

place of her own." He doesn't look at me, just continuing to stare out the window.

"You're a real asshole, you know that?"

"Yeah. I know." He drags his fingers through his hair and turns to meet my gaze. For the first time since he told me about the pregnancy, I actually see remorse in his eyes. "Will you let her stay?"

"I'm not going to kick her out, if that's what you're asking."

He gives a small nod, his expression relaxing slightly. "I do care about her."

"You've got a funny way of showing it."

Ignoring me, he continues. "She's different than the other girls I've been with. There's something about her. You know?"

Yeah, I know. I saw it the first time I laid eyes on her.

Travis rubs his temples.

"I can't bail you out of this one. You know that. Whether you like it or not, Layla and this kid are part of your life now." *And mine.*

His jaw tightens, but he nods.

"I'm not saying you have to marry her—"

"Yeah, that's not going to happen." He stands abruptly, clearly agitated. "I'm going to have a shower."

"Travis." The command in my voice stops him. "This doesn't have to be a bad thing."

He snorts. "You can say that because it's not your life she's fucking with. If you want her to have the kid so bad, then you take care of it."

My chest tightens, and something stirs inside of me. Yeah, it's that damn caveman again, growling to comply with Travis' request.

You take care of it.

Watching Travis skulk up the stairs, I know there's

nothing I can say to change his mind. And there's a small part of me that doesn't want him to. Because if, or when, he walks away, I have no intention of just offering her the deal he's laid out.

I have a deal of my own. One that will finally make her mine.

CHAPTER 6

LAYLA

$\mathcal{T}$he house is empty when I come home from work, which isn't that unusual. If Travis isn't throwing a party, he's typically out at a club, or at one of his stoner buddies' houses. But the minute I walk into the kitchen and see the folded note on the kitchen table with my name scribbled on it, my insides clench.

I place my purse on the chair and pick it up, slowly unfolding it.

LAYLA,
  I can't do this.
  I'm sorry.
  Stay in the house as long as you need.
  - Travis

THAT'S IT. No long apology. No excuses. Just the cold, brutal fact that he doesn't want to be a part of his child's life.

My fingers flutter over my still flat stomach, and I let out a long uneven breath. When I left for work this morning, I never thought he would just up and leave.

"So, that's it," I mutter, feeling the first pricks of tears at the backs of my eyes. I swipe them away angrily.

I don't know why I'm crying. Travis was, at best, a friend, but there was never anything more between us. Just one stupid night that meant nothing.

And he's right. He isn't mature enough to be a father. Maybe he never will be.

I flinch when I hear the front door open and shut, and the footsteps behind me.

"Layla?" Carter's deep voice is full of concern.

I take a deep breath and let it out slowly before turning around.

Carter's face tightens, and he takes the remaining steps that separate us. "What's wrong?"

Not trusting my voice, I don't say anything. I just hand him the note.

His eyes graze over the words, and his expression goes from concerned to furious.

"Fuck." His fist balls over the note, and for a second it looks like he's ready to hit something. A few deep breaths, and he turns back to me. "I didn't think he'd leave so quickly. I'm sorry."

"It is what it is." I try to act casual, like I'm not completely freaking out inside. But I have no clue what I'm going to do.

I have some money in savings. Enough for a down payment for first and last month's rent somewhere, if it's not too expensive. But neither of my jobs, waitressing at the diner or managing the bookstore, have any medical coverage.

And then there are all the other expenses that come with babies.

I rub my eyes with my palms and shake my head. There's still time for me to think about all that. Right now, I just have to figure out where I'm going to live.

"If I can stay here for a few more days, it'll give me enough time to—"

"I'm not kicking you out." He stares at me with all the broody intenseness that makes my knees go weak.

Silence stretches between us, and I feel like there's something that he wants to say, but he doesn't. What I wouldn't give to have him wrap those strong arms around me. To comfort me. But I know that would be a really bad idea.

Just being in the same room with him is hard enough. Adding any physical contact would be a temptation I don't have the strength for right now.

I sit down on the kitchen chair and place my hands on the table.

"I can't stay here."

"Why not?" He pulls out the chair beside me and straddles it, arms resting on the back, his blue eyes watchful.

"Because it's your place. With Travis gone—"

"It changes nothing."

"It changes everything." I hold his gaze, trying not to flinch at the intensity of it. "I appreciate you wanting to help, but this is already weird between us."

"It doesn't have to be. With my job, I'm gone for weeks, sometimes months at a time. Plus..." His jaw tenses, his mouth tightening. "Once Travis gets his head out of his ass and realizes what he's giving up, he'll be back."

Not likely.

I shrug.

Carter's mouth tightens, and he breathes out heavily

through his nose. "This is your home, for as long as you need it to be."

"You don't have to do this."

"Yeah. I do." He frowns. "You were right earlier when you said Travis and I aren't very close. It's my fault. I left him alone when our parents died. If I'd done things differently, maybe he wouldn't be such a self-absorbed asshole."

I can't help but smile at the fierceness in his tone. Travis hadn't spoken much about his parents. I knew they were dead, that they'd died in a head-on collision, but that's all he had said.

"What happened to them?"

Carter lets out a long sigh before answering. "They were in a car accident. My mom was killed instantly. She wasn't wearing her seatbelt, and ..." He looks up at the ceiling and shakes his head. "She was ejected from the car. Broke her neck on impact."

"I'm so sorry."

"Both Travis and my dad were rushed to the hospital—"

"Travis was with them?" He hadn't told me that part.

"He had a few fractured ribs, a concussion, and a broken arm. He was lucky. If you saw the wreckage..." He drags his fingers through his dark hair. "It's a miracle anyone survived."

"And your dad?"

"They pronounced him brain-dead at the hospital. When I got there, I was given the option of unplugging him, or keeping him hooked up to the machines." His eyes go distant and his lips tighten in a thin line. "I knew my dad wouldn't have wanted to live like that. So I made the decision."

"God, that must have been terrible."

"Yeah. But what was worse was when Travis came out of surgery and found out what I'd done. He never forgave me for it."

"How old was he?"

"Seventeen. Not old enough to be alone, but I left him anyways. I was consumed by my own life. My own needs. I practically left him on his own after that. I made sure he had everything he needed, and cleaned up his messes whenever he called for help. But looking back, I think that only made things worse. What he needed was family."

I can see the guilt in his eyes, and hear the love for his brother in his voice, but there are some mistakes that can never be fixed, especially if one person isn't willing to forgive.

"Have you told him that?"

"Probably not as gently as I could have." His lips twist up slightly. "Travis and I have a complicated relationship."

"That seems to be the only type he's capable of."

Carter grunts. "You may be right."

We sit in silence for a few moments, both caught up in our own thoughts.

"I'm sorry for the way he treated you." His gaze is on me again.

"You can't blame yourself for his actions. No matter how many mistakes you may have made, he's his own person."

"True. But I can make sure that his child is taken care of. That you..." He reaches out and takes my hand, making my entire body turn into an inferno. "Are taken care of."

"I'm..." I swallow, finding it difficult to concentrate on anything but his touch. "*We're* not your responsibility."

"Until Travis comes back, you are." He lets his hand rest on mine, his gaze so intense that despite the warmth that floods through me, a shiver races down my back.

The way he looks at me makes me forget everything.

Who I am.

Who he is.

That I'm carrying his brother's baby.

My body practically hums with the need for his touch. And the protective, almost possessive way he's looking at me right now makes my insides melt. Makes me want more. More than I can ever have.

Warning bells blare.

Danger. Danger. Run as fast as you can.

I pull my hand away and stand.

"Thank you for letting me stay here for now."

I don't wait for his response, because I need to get as far away from him as possible, to clear my head.

Maybe I'm reading him all wrong. Maybe the touch and the look are just him. There's no denying the man oozes sex appeal. And my hormones are all over the place. Maybe he's just trying to be the responsible brother, cleaning up Travis' mess.

I shut my bedroom door, locking it behind me.

Yeah, that's all it is. Nothing more. Because what man in his right mind would be interested in a woman carrying another man's baby? Especially when that man is his brother.

Unless he's just interested in sex.

But then, there are a million women out there that I'm sure would be more than willing to jump into bed with an incredibly hot ex-NHL player.

Lying down on my bed, I curl into a ball and close my eyes. But the minute I do, Carter's handsome face is there, staring at me with those fuck-me eyes.

Damn him for being so incredibly sexy – and sweet.

That was the real kicker. If he was a jackass like his brother, it would be easy—well, not completely easy, but easier—not to think about him. But under all Carter's brood-iness, and the dark scowl he wears like a uniform, is a man who cares deeply about others.

A man that I could easily fall for.

CHAPTER 7

CARTER

"I'm not reneging on my contract. I just need a week to deal with a family situation that's come up."

"Christ, Carter. We're right in the middle of playoffs." My boss's voice is near hysterical, and I can't really blame him. "I need you here. I need you doing the damn job I'm paying you for."

Paying me shit for.

"One week," I barter.

"Four days. I want you in New York on Monday."

I hang up and curse under my breath. I don't need this damn job. I have more than enough money in savings, and even with constantly bailing Travis' ass out of debt, I can get by on the interest.

But this job is the only thing that keeps me connected to my old life.

The magazine I write for is a piece of shit. But it gets me

48

through the doors of pretty much any sporting event I want to attend. And it got me off the couch and out of the depression that had been my life since my injury.

But right now, the last thing I want to think about is leaving.

Travis isn't answering his cell. Knowing him, he probably trashed the damn thing so I wouldn't have a way of tracking him down and beating the shit out of him.

Unlike Layla, I didn't get a note, just a voicemail telling me he was sorry and not to look for him. Of all the asshole things Travis has done, this has to be the worst.

The soft padding of footsteps travels down the hall, and I hear Layla open the door to her room, then shut it.

Fuck if I know what I'm going to do about her.

There's no way in hell I'm letting her leave. I was serious when I told her this is her home now. My name might be on the mortgage, but I'd always intended on giving it to Travis once he got his shit together. But that doesn't look like it's going to happen. At least, not in the foreseeable future.

It's only right that the house goes to his kid, or to the mother of his kid.

The thought of just giving it to her, signing the papers in her name, crosses my mind. It would be the cleanest solution. Layla and the child would be taken care of.

But then what?

I'd go back to New York. Travel. Work. Maybe come and visit once or twice a year – if she let me.

The thought twists my stomach.

My parents would be rolling over in their graves right now if they could see what's become of Travis...of me...of our once happy, normal family.

Family was everything to them. They poured their hearts and souls into making sure we knew we were loved, that we belonged. Sometimes, I think Travis forgets all of that. That his memories are twisted and distorted because of his pain.

Layla's door creaks open again, and I can hear her tiptoeing down the hall towards the bathroom, then the sound of the shower turning on.

I groan at the thought of her naked only a room away. I remember the heat in her soft brown eyes when I'd kissed her in the bar, and again when she'd seen me for the first time the other night.

The connection is still there – maybe even stronger than before.

But this whole situation is one big cluster-fuck.

I should let my lawyers handle it. Go back to New York and not look back. That would be the smart thing to do.

Who is she to me anyways? The only thing that connects us is an unforgettable kiss and a child that isn't even mine.

But damn, I wish it was. I drag my fingers through my hair, not knowing where that thought came from.

Sure, the woman is gorgeous, and there's no denying the chemistry between us. There's something about her that makes me want to protect her.

But she's pregnant with my brother's baby.

Getting involved, more than just financially, wouldn't just be stupid, it would be emotional suicide.

And I just finally stepped back from the edge of darkness. The last thing I need in my life is more bullshit.

Layla. Me. It can't work.

And yet, even as I think it, I know I've already made up my mind. The moment I knew Travis was gone, I'd made my decision.

I'm not going to walk away.

The inner caveman inside of me claimed her months ago – the first time I saw her, and the first time I tasted her.

My cock hardens at the memory, my body pulsing with

the need to fill her. Imagining those big, innocent eyes watching me as I fulfill all my dark, wicked fantasies. I've never wanted to lose myself to a woman as much as I do Layla.

Sick as it is, that's my reality.

But she's going to need time.

The last thing I want is to scare her. And from the way she tiptoes around me, trying not to meet my gaze, I know that wouldn't be difficult to do.

I'm not normally a patient man, but I know I'm going to have to be with her.

Despite my better judgement telling me to run in the opposite direction, I know exactly what I have to do to make her mine. I'm a man who would go to any lengths to get what he wants. And I've never wanted anything more than I want her.

CHAPTER 8

LAYLA

I stare at the blank screen in front of me like I've done for the past twenty minutes. But the harder I try to think about a story to write, the more my brain becomes a fuzz of static.

Nothing.

Frustrated, I slam the laptop cover down and push my chair back.

It's pointless. I can't write.

I grab a paperback off the shelf and lay down on my bed. But a few pages in, I'm ready to toss it across the room, because I'm so sick and tired of reading about other people's love stories. For once in my life, I want my own.

My stomach grumbles, and I glance at the electric clock by my bed.

It's almost midnight, but I can't sleep.

I'm restless. Not just because of the whole Travis leaving

shenanigans, but because I'm constantly aware of the sexy, tattooed bad boy that's currently living under my roof.

Rather, *his* roof.

Travis hadn't told me that his brother owned the house. But it makes sense, considering Travis can't seem to hold a job, let alone pay a mortgage.

I roll out of bed and slowly open my bedroom door, peeking out like I'm ten years old again, expecting to get reprimanded for being out of bed past my bedtime.

All the lights are off. Even the one under Carter's door.

As silently as I can, I tiptoe down the stairs towards the kitchen, opening the fridge and pulling out the carton of chocolate milk.

I'm in the middle of pouring a glass when the lights flick on.

With my already frayed nerves, I startle, and both the glass and the carton drop from my hands, bouncing off the kitchen counter and spewing milk everywhere before landing on the floor. The glass shatters in a hundred little pieces by my feet.

"Shit," Carter curses, rushing towards me. Then he demands, "Don't move."

I hear him, but it's as if my feet have a mind of their own. I quickly take a step back, yelping when a piece of glass slices into my heel.

"Damn it. I told you not to move." With the agility of a trained boxer, he maneuvers through the broken glass and chocolate milk. I don't know what he's doing until his hands are on my waist, lifting me up and then plopping me down on the counter. He points a finger at me. "Stay."

I swallow hard and nod, now rendered speechless because I finally take in his appearance.

Wearing only a pair of navy pajama bottoms that hang

low on his hips, his muscular chest is bare, exposing all the glorious patterns I haven't seen before.

He's even more ripped than I'd imagined. While Travis was toned and on the thinner side, Carter is all rippling muscle.

As he sweeps up the glass, he glances up at me and catches me staring, and his blue eyes go dark.

I want to look away, but I can't. It's like he's got some superpower to control my body, infusing it with heat in a single glance. I shift my position on the counter, feeling all that heat go straight between my legs.

His lips twist up just slightly, and I swear he reads my thoughts.

Heat suffuses my cheeks, giving me the strength to look away.

"You scared me," I say, breaking the tense silence between us.

"I came down to get a drink," he grumbles, dumping the glass in the trashcan.

More strained silence.

When he's finished mopping up the mess, he pulls out a clean dishtowel from the drawer, then runs it under the tap.

He's beside me, and only a few inches separate us. Wringing out the towel, he looks at me, then down at my legs, which I realize now are bare and splattered in chocolate milk.

"Which foot did you hurt?"

"My right."

"Let me see." His expression is stoic, hard and unyielding.

I lift my leg, and he captures my ankle in his large hand. All my muscles tense as I try to control the shiver that races down my back and through my limbs.

He crouches slightly to inspect the damage, then gently presses the wet dishtowel against my heel.

"It looks like a clean cut. I don't see any glass. Where's your first aid kit?"

I nod at the cupboard beside the fridge. "Second shelf."

He pulls it out and rummages through it until he finds a Band-Aid, then moves back to me.

"Hold this." He hands bandage to me, then moves back to the sink and rinses out the towel.

His nostrils flare slightly when he turns back to me, and he takes one of my legs in his hands again, and starts to wipe it down with the dishtowel.

"What are you doing?"

"You have milk all over you."

"Oh. Right." It's a stupid thing to say, but then his touch does that to me – makes me say and do senseless things.

One callused hand cups the back of my calf gently.

I can't think.

Can't breathe.

All I can do is watch him as he drags the towel in slow, deliberate movements across my lower leg.

Energy spins between us, filling the space with a heat that makes my body feel feverish.

I need to get away from him. Because with every small touch, he's distorting my judgement, making me feels things I have no business feeling.

A soft hum vibrates in my throat, and I pray to God that he doesn't hear it.

His gaze remains on my legs, lifting the other one and spending just as much time, if not more, on cleaning it.

When he finally releases me, every cell in my body is vibrating, crying out for more of his touch.

Holy hell, the man is hot.

And sweet.

And so freaking off limits.

He tosses the towel in the sink, and then looks up at me,

one palm out. After a few seconds, one eyebrow goes up. "The Band-Aid."

"Right." Crap. I hand it to him, watching as he takes the wrapper off, gently placing it on my heel.

His fingers linger on my ankle, his gaze once again on my legs.

"All better." As light as his words are, his expression remains dark.

"Thank you." I swallow past the lump in the back of my throat.

He nods, and his hands go around my waist again, lifting me and slowly sliding me down his body until my feet hit the floor.

There's no hiding the huge erection he's sporting, or the fact that it's digging into my belly now.

I lick my lips and look up at him, lust warring with fear.

"Go to bed, Layla." His voice is a deep, barely contained growl.

A warning.

He takes a small step back, but from his expression, I can see it takes all his strength to do it.

I do the only sensible thing I can think of. I turn and walk away from the hulking temptation, knowing I'm going to need to keep a lot more distance between us if I'm going to survive him being here much longer.

CHAPTER 9

CARTER

I try to give Layla space, which isn't hard, because I realize pretty quickly that she's juggling two jobs as well as volunteering a few hours each week at the local animal shelter.

That, and she's avoiding me.

She's going through a lot. I get it. Which is why I'm not pushing things. At least, not yet.

Sitting on the living room couch, I rub the back of my neck and read through the piece I'm currently working on, scratching out the last line that I wrote.

The whole article is shit. Mostly because I can't focus. The only thing I can think about is Layla, and how I'm going to play this.

Slow and steady. It's not my typical speed, but I'm going to have to be patient. There's more at stake than just getting her in my bed – which will happen.

But what I really want is her trust, and eventually her heart.

Two things that I can tell she keeps safely guarded.

I've been here three days and I still know barely anything about her. What I do know is that she's got her walls up, and it's going to take a fucking militia to tear them down.

I crumple the paper I'm working on and toss it on the coffee table beside my laptop.

Work is on me, pressuring me to come back to New York. I've used the family emergency excuse, but I have to leave soon.

The creak of footsteps on the stairs has my gaze jerking up.

Wearing black pants that hug her curvy hips, and a loose-fitting blouse that's buttoned up to her neck, Layla strides into the room, a look of determination tightening her features.

My sexy librarian.

The things I'm going to do to her when I finally get her in my bed.

"Here." She leans over and places a pile of bills on the coffee table beside my laptop. "I'm twenty short, but I'll get it to you by tomorrow."

She turns and starts to walk away.

I frown down at the bills, not understanding.

"Layla, wait." My voice is gruffer than intended. It always is with her, even though I keep reminding myself to be gentle.

She stops, her back turned to me, and her shoulders rise and fall on a heavy breath before turning to look at me.

"What is this?" I pick up the bills, which, after a quick count, is around five hundred dollars.

"Rent."

Is she serious?

"I'm not charging you to stay here."

"It's what I was paying before, and it's less than I'd pay anywhere else. So, take it. Please."

There's something in her tone that stops me from arguing.

"All right." I put the money back on the table. "If that's what you want."

"I do." Her expression is stoic, but even though she tries to hide it, there's a flash of emotion in her eyes when she finally meets my gaze. Her cheeks turn a cute shade of pink.

That's right, sweetheart. You're mine. Your body knows it. I'm just waiting for your heart and mind to catch up.

She licks her lips and looks down at the floor, as if she wants to say something.

"What's wrong?"

"I was wondering..." She shifts nervously from one foot to the other.

God, she's fucking beautiful. She draws her plump lower lip between her teeth and I have to suppress the groan that rumbles in my throat.

"Just ask, Layla."

"I'm not sure if you noticed, but the washing machine doesn't work. I don't mind using a Laundromat, but it might be easier..."

No I hadn't noticed, because I had my own clothes dry cleaned.

"I'll buy a new one today." Frustration bubbles inside of me. I'd given Travis money for a new one two months ago. God only knows what he spent it on.

"Thanks." She gives me a stiff smile, then walks to the door.

"Layla." Her name sounds like a growl on my lips, because no matter how hard I try to suppress my need for her, the minute she walks into my line of vision, I'm instantly rock hard. And right now, seeing that sweet little ass of hers walking away is killing me.

She stops with her hand on the doorknob and looks at me, her eyes wide.

Does she know how much I want her? I doubt it. Because if she had even the slightest clue of the things I want to do to her, she wouldn't be walking away. She'd be running.

"Whatever you need, don't be afraid to ask." I say the last word with emphasis. "Ever."

There's reservation in her eyes, but she nods before shutting the door behind her.

I slam my laptop shut and head upstairs to the shower, and my rock hard cock is in my hand before the water is even lukewarm. My balls are drawn painfully tight against my body, my seed begging to be spilled.

Having her under the same roof as me, and not being able to touch her, is painful. Brutally painful.

Patience, I remind myself, placing a hand on the shower wall and stroking myself to the vision of Layla's mouth stretched around my cock, her gorgeous eyes looking up at me with the trust and uninhibited desire I long to see.

Soon.

Very, very soon.

She will be mine.

Heart.

Body.

And mind.

CHAPTER 10

LAYLA

"Y ou look exhausted," Kira says when she comes into the bookstore, half an hour late for her shift as usual.

I should never have hired her knowing how unreliable she is. But she needed the job after being let go at her last one.

"I haven't been sleeping much," I mutter, shelfing the book in my hand.

Kira shrugs off her jacket and throws it behind the counter, then comes to help me with the new arrivals. "Still stressed about Travis leaving?"

If only that was the reason.

Lying awake at night, knowing that only a few feet and a door separate Carter and I, hasn't just been hard, it's been fricking torture.

I don't know how much longer I can take having him

around. But so far, he's given no indication that he has any intention of leaving. Ever.

I'm nervous and on edge all the time. Not because he's done anything wrong, but because he's done everything right. My nerves are fueled by my awareness of him.

He's always there, even when he isn't.

His scent.

His things.

They're constantly around, reminding me of everything I can't have.

And the way he looks at me, like he's practically undressing me every time I walk into a room, makes my body respond in ways it has no right to.

I wonder if he'll still look at me like that when I start to show. When my stomach is so big that I can't even see my feet. Placing my hand on my still flat stomach, it seems like such a long way away. But I know how quickly time passes, and soon there will be a constant physical reminder of what really separates us.

Maybe that'll be a good thing. Maybe it'll finally make this torture bearable.

"You seem distracted," Kira says, frowning at me. "You want to talk?"

"Not really."

Kira gives a sad, knowing smile, but doesn't push. She's good like that. Knows her boundaries.

I love her, even if she is one of the worst employees I've ever hired.

"You should go home. I can close up. It looks like it's going to be another slow night."

Usually, I'd say no. But I'm exhausted and all I want to do is sleep. Well, that's not exactly true. There are a lot of things I want to do. And all of them involve Carter Bennet.

But sleep, and maybe a warm bath, will have to suffice.

CHAPTER 11

CARTER

*U*pstairs, I pass Layla's room. The door is open a few inches, enough that I can see in. Everything is neat, and perfectly ordered. Even the damn bed is made. And not just a quick toss of the covers, but perfectly made, like they do in hotels, with the creases and the folded edges.

Another weird quirk I want to know more about.

I push the door open wider, breathing in her soft scent.

I know I shouldn't be in here. But I want to know more about her, and right now she isn't exactly offering many details.

The room is pretty bare. Other than her books, which are piled neatly around the room, and an ancient laptop that looks like it was built in the Middle Ages, there's nothing that really makes it hers.

No pictures, no little trinkets. Just books. So many damn books.

Romance.

Mysteries.

Biographies.

Classics.

She even has one of those electronic eBook readers.

A tattered copy of War and Peace sits on her nightstand. I pick it up and shake my head. I'm pretty sure I haven't read the equivalent number of pages in my entire life, but it's obvious that this book has been read and reread several times.

I'm about to put it back when I see the edge of a photo sticking out. I flip open the ragged cover and pull out the picture. A family portrait. One of those posed ones that makes everyone look awkward and depressed. The father is in a suit, his expression overly serious as he stares into the camera with a self-righteous expression. The mother's expression isn't much softer, but it's the grip on the little girl's shoulder that draws my eye. Like claws, her fingers seem to dig into the child's flesh painfully.

Layla is about nine or ten in the picture. She has the same light brown eyes. Her hair is a lighter shade of brown, pulled painfully tight in a braid. And she looks completely miserable.

Protectiveness swells inside me.

"You shouldn't be in here." Stealthily, Layla comes up behind me and grabs the picture out of my hand.

Shit.

"I'm sorry. The door was open..." Not an excuse. I hand her the book. "Sorry. You're right."

She glares up at me, then quickly tucks the picture back in the book and clutches it to her chest.

"Were you checking up on me?"

"No." I rub the back of my neck.

"Because I have nothing to hide," she says defensively.

"I didn't think you did. I'm sorry, really. It won't happen again. This is your space and I shouldn't have been in here."

"No. You shouldn't have been." She turns her back on me and tosses a bag of what looks like more books on her bed.

I know why she works so much. To pay for her damn reading habit.

The thought gives me an idea of something I'd like to do for her. The basement has been left unfinished for years. Just a cement floor with insulation in the walls. But the space is big enough for a den, or more specifically, a library slash office, where she could go to read and write.

"Did you want something?" Layla's gaze is narrowed on me, her arms crossed over her chest.

Yeah, for you to trust me, sweetheart. But the way she's looking at me now, like I'm her enemy, I know that's not going to happen any time soon.

"I know it's none of my business, but have you told them?" I nod at the novel in her hands, the one that holds the old photograph of her family.

"My parents?" She chuckles darkly, but I can see the pain she's trying to hide behind her anger. "No."

Something protective billows in my chest, rising up in the middle of it, and I have to clamp my mouth shut on my next question, because I can see she doesn't want to talk about them.

Her eyes dart around the room, and I get the feeling that she'd do just about anything to avoid the conversation.

I want to wrap her in my arms and tell her everything will be okay. Instead, I change the subject. "The new washing machine should be here tomorrow. And I also fixed the leak in the shower."

There's a small break in her armor, before it goes back up again.

"Thank you. It'll make it easier once…" She glances away and shifts nervously.

"Once the baby comes," I add, allowing her to put a voice to the thing Travis wanted her to hide.

"Yeah."

"You can talk about it with me. *Not* talking about it isn't going to make it go away."

"I know that." She frowns at me. "It's just awkward with you."

I take a step towards her, and her eyes widen slightly.

"It doesn't have to be." Another step closer, and I see her swallow hard, her gaze dropping to my mouth.

"Everything about this—"She gestures around the room with her free hand, the other one still clutching the damn book against her chest like a shield, "—is awkward."

"Because I kissed you?" I'm standing in front of her now, so close I can practically feel the warmth of her body radiating off her.

She sucks in a breath. "Twice."

"Yeah, twice. And I wanted to do it a hell of a lot more times." I reach out and stroke my knuckles across her cheek. "I still do."

"Carter—"

I brush the pad of my thumb across her lips, silencing her protest. "I know you're not ready."

"I tried calling," she says softly, a slight tremble in her voice. "But the number you gave me…"

"I'd just switched numbers. When I realized my mistake, I tried to track you down, but you were already gone."

"Oh." Her frown deepens.

"But I didn't stop thinking about you, hoping one day we'd meet again."

She laughs humorlessly. "I'm sure you never thought it'd be under these circumstances."

"No." I match her frown and cup her cheek, the gesture far more intimate than I'd intended, but I can't seem to pull away. "But I'll work with what I've got."

She licks her lips, and I see a small flare of hope in her eyes. But just as quickly, it's gone, replaced by uncertainty and fear.

"I can't do this."

I lean down and press my lips to her forehead, feeling her shiver.

"Then I guess I'll have to wait until you can."

CHAPTER 12

LAYLA

*W*hen Carter is gone, I touch my lips where his thumb had been a few minutes before. My body still buzzes with electricity, and my brain is spinning with what he just said.

Then I guess I'll have to wait until you can.

A million questions blare in my head. Questions I'm too much of a coward to ask.

Like, why me? Why now? If it's just sex he wants, he can get it anywhere. And if it's more, which I can't imagine is likely, is he really willing to stick around when I'm going to have his brother's baby?

This whole situation isn't just awkward, it's insane.

I flip open the cover of War and Peace and pull out the old photo, frowning when I run my fingers over my mother's stern face.

God, despite everything, there are some days when I really miss her.

Today is one of them.

What I wouldn't give to crawl into my old bed and have her stroke my hair and sing me to sleep like she used to do when I was little. But that will never happen. To them, I might as well be dead, because there's no going home. Ever.

I put the picture back, snorting when I think about what they would say if they saw me now. I can only imagine the horrified look on my mom's face if she ever saw Carter with all his tattoos.

Tattoos are the devil's mark. That's what my parents believed.

Seven years away from them and I can still hear their voices in my head, constantly criticizing, always condemning

Still dressed in my work clothes, I pull back the sheets and crawl into bed, wrapping my arms around my chest and wishing it was Carter's strong arms holding me, comforting me.

Don't be delusional, Layla.

If I allow him in and drop my guard, I know I'll never survive when he walks away. And there's no doubt in my mind that he *will* walk away.

As good as his intentions are, and as strong as the attraction is between us, I'm still carrying another man's child.

Better to keep my walls up. Keep the boundaries defined that I've already put in place. Remember why it's dangerous to trust anyone.

Sucking in a shaky breath, I pinch my eyes shut and try to ignore the hollowness inside of me. The vacant spot that yearns to be filled.

He'll destroy me if I let him.

It's better to be alone.

But I've always been alone, and somedays it's just too much.

My parents weren't able to conceive again after they had

me, so from a young age, with no siblings around, I learned how to be on my own. It's one of the reasons I love reading so much. Books aren't just an escape, they're my connection to people – even if those people aren't real.

Yeah, I'm used to being alone.

But it doesn't make it any less lonely.

I pull the comforter over my shoulders. I'm exhausted. Too tired to think. Almost too tired to feel. But as sleep pulls me into its cradle of darkness, only one face fills my dreams.

Carter.

CHAPTER 13

LAYLA

"Good, you're home," Carter calls out from the kitchen when I walk in the house. "I made dinner."

Frowning, I toss my purse on the table by the front door and follow the scent of garlic and basil. The house smells delicious, and my mouth waters. Still, I'm not sure what to think when I walk into the kitchen and see the table set, with fresh rolls, silverware, and real fabric napkins.

Carter hovers over the stove, stirring a large silver pot, then moves to the counter and starts to dice vegetables, his big, tattooed hands working with the skilled precision of a gourmet chef.

Is there anything he can't do?

The sight of this beast of a man making dinner isn't just sexy, it's purely erotic.

I rub my sweaty hands on my jeans and try to get a grip on my hormones.

"What is this?" I ask cautiously, aware of how tainted I sound.

"Dinner." He gives me a crooked grin, nodding at the table. "Sit."

"You cook?"

"I've been told I make a mean plate of spaghetti." He places a heaping plate of pasta with Bolognese sauce in front of me.

"This looks great. Thank you." I can't remember the last time someone made me a meal. Even when I lived with Kira, her idea of cooking was ordering takeout.

Carter limps slightly when he moves around the table, and I can't help but notice the way he favors one leg. Placing the salad on the table, he pulls out a chair and sits down across from me.

I can feel his gaze on me as I take the first bite.

"It's really good," I say truthfully.

"It's my mother's recipe." He passes me the salad.

"You made the sauce?" To say I'm impressed is an understatement.

"Yeah. It's pretty easy." A sad smile plays on his beautiful lips. "She used to make everything from scratch. Even grew her own vegetables in the backyard."

"She sounds like an amazing woman."

"She was."

We eat in silence for a few minutes, but the awkwardness between us isn't as strong as it was, and I actually enjoy the few quiet moments just being with him. It's nice. Better than nice. It's...*intimate*.

Him.

Me.

Dinner.

It seems like such a normal thing.

But nothing about this is normal, I remind myself.

"You played hockey, right? Travis mentioned that you used to be sort of a big shot."

He looks at me with an odd expression, one that I can't interpret.

"Yeah, I used to be." The words drip with bitterness. "I was injured a few years ago. Shattered my knee. Couldn't play after that."

"I'm sorry." I look down at my plate, wishing I hadn't brought it up.

"Do you watch hockey?"

"No." I shake my head. "Sports were never my thing."

"You preferred reading." He smiles, exposing the dimple in his cheek.

I nod. "So, what do you do now? Travis never told me."

"I'm a sports journalist for a crappy little magazine in New York called The Shutout."

I place my fork on my plate and look at him, probably bug-eyed, because that was the last thing I expected for him to say. "You're a writer?"

"Not really." He shrugs. "I just report on the games. It's mostly stats. I wouldn't call myself a writer. Not like you. You've actually written something substantial."

"I told you, it's not very good—"

"Maybe. But if it's your dream, then you should pursue it."

"I think I've had enough rejection letters for one lifetime."

He clears his throat and attempts an accent when he says, "Don't fear failure. Not failure, but low aim, is the crime. In great attempts, it is glorious even to fail."

I raise an eyebrow and laugh. "Yoda?"

"Bruce Lee." He chuckles and pushes a casual hand through his hair. "I used to have a poster with those words in my room when I was a kid."

"Well, it seemed to work for you. You got everything you wanted."

"Not everything," he says, his expression serious and trained on me.

Oh.

I lick my lips and look away. "I guess we're not meant to get everything we want."

He doesn't respond, but I can feel his eyes on me as I move the spaghetti across my plate with my fork.

"You should eat before it gets cold," he says, the mood between us changing once again.

The rest of the meal is filled with small talk.

As dark and broody as he comes across, Carter is actually very easy to talk to. I learn that he grew up in a large Victorian-style house not far from here. And that despite his bad boy image, he really was the Golden Boy. Somehow, he managed to still do well in school, and even got a college diploma while juggling hockey.

The way he talks about his parents makes my heart ache. They seemed to have had the perfect family, at least until the accident.

Now, all Carter has left is Travis – and he's gone, because of me.

Guilt settles in my chest.

"I'll wash the dishes," I say, standing and taking my plate to the sink.

"There's this crazy contraption that actually does that for you. I think it's called a dishwasher," he teases, placing his dirty dishes on the counter.

I shake my head and tell him the unfortunate news. "Yeah, that's broken, too."

"Shit. Seriously? What the hell did Travis spend the money on that I gave him then?"

"Do you really want to know?" I lift my brows at him.

"Probably not." He shakes his head.

"Here." I hand him a dishtowel. "You can dry and put them away."

"I'll order a new dishwasher tomorrow." He leans with his back against the counter and watches me wash the first dish.

"I don't mind doing the dishes by hand. I actually find it relaxing. Reminds me of when I was a kid, helping my mom after dinner. Things were so much simpler then."

"Yeah, sometimes it sucks getting older."

"Sometimes," I mumble, handing him a clean dish.

His fingers brush over mine when he takes it from me, and without warning, heat spreads through my body.

One touch, and I light up like I've been struck by lightning. Tingles coat my skin, and a rush of desire spreads through me like wildfire.

I've never felt anything like I feel when I'm with him.

He oozes maleness. Strength and power.

And even though I have no right to feel it, I feel safe when I'm with him. Like everything will be okay.

It's both exhilarating and terrifying at the same time.

I suck in a few deep breaths, doing my best to ignore my pounding heart while tight knots of panic swirl around in my stomach.

My breathing must have stopped, because all of a sudden there are small little white lights in my vision and everything else starts to go dark. The floor shifts under me, and I drop the plate I'm holding back in the sink.

"Layla." His arms are around me instantly, steadying me.

Dizziness assaults me, but I'm still fully aware of the hardness of his body, the warmth of his hands holding me. One is on my waist, the other runs up my back until it's cupping the back of my head.

"I'm…okay."

He doesn't let go. "Are you feeling sick?"

"Just a little lightheaded." I can't help but lean into his touch. "It's...normal. Pregnancy hormones or something."

He frowns and exhales heavily. "Still. You should go in to see your doctor."

"I'll tell her about it at my next appointment."

He's still touching me.

I know I should move. Take a step back. But it's like the world around us has stopped.

Almost involuntarily, or at least that's what I tell myself, I place my hands on his broad chest. I can feel every hard ridge of his body, every muscle as it tenses under my touch.

I have to tilt my chin to look up at him, and when I meet his intense gaze, another thrill shoots through my body.

For a long second, there are no words.

Just feelings.

Raw.

Intense.

Wrong.

Feelings.

I shouldn't be touching him. Or feeling the things I do. It isn't right.

"I think I need to lie down."

His lips twitch down, then he takes a step back and slowly releases me. "I'll finish the dishes."

"Thank you for dinner."

He nods, but his back is to me before I can say anything else.

"I have to leave for a few weeks," he says, when I start to walk away.

"Oh." Disappointment floods through me, even though I knew he wouldn't be here forever. He has a job that requires him to travel, and an apartment in New York. Of course he has to leave.

This is why I need to stay away from him. Why I can't let my emotions get involved.

The muscles in his back bunch under his t-shirt as he scrubs a plate and places it in the rack beside the sink. "I'll leave my cell in case you need anything."

"A new dishwasher," I tease, hoping to lighten the tension between us.

He gives a small grunt and looks over his shoulder at me, his expression unreadable. "I'll order one tomorrow."

With a frustrated sigh, I make my way to my bedroom. Maybe it's just as well that he leaves. I can't afford to lose control, or act on my growing need for him. The longer he stays, the more I'll get used to having him around.

CHAPTER 14

LAYLA

"*W*hen does he come back?" Kira asks, plopping down on the couch beside me, her strawberry blonde hair twisted in a messy bun on top of her head.

"He said a few weeks, but I don't know. I lived here for almost four months with Travis before Carter ever came by. Maybe he just plans on staying away."

"Would that be so bad?"

I shrug. "It would make things easier."

"You still like him, don't you?" Her brows raise.

"No." I shake my head. *Lie.* I'm twisted up in knots over him. "I mean, I can't. He's Travis' brother. How weird would that be?"

"Weird," Kira admits. "But it's not like Travis is around."

True. But he could come back. It's not likely, but there's always the chance. Travis doesn't have a possessive streak in his body, but I doubt he'd be pleased if he came home and found me sleeping with his brother.

"It's your life, Layla. You can't let what other people think dictate what you do. I thought you'd have learned that by now."

"It's not just what people would think."

"You're worried he's going to bail on you, like Travis."

"Maybe. Yes." I shrug. "It's just every time I'm in the same room with him, I feel…" God. I don't even know what I feel. I just…feel. So many damn things.

Nervous.

Happy.

Safe.

And the worst, lust.

It's foolish to even think about it.

But he makes me want things I'd never wanted before. Craving something I can never let myself have.

"He's just so…" *Confident. Sexy. Strong. Gorgeous.*

"Yeah. You're not into him at all," Kira teases, obviously reading my thoughts on my face.

I sigh heavily. "I can't afford to be."

Her lips tug down and she shakes her head, her expression suddenly serious. There's something else on her mind. Something she's been wanting to say since she got here. I can see it in her eyes.

"What?"

"Nothing." She fidgets with the throw pillow she's holding in her lap.

I know the look she's giving me, and it's definitely not nothing.

"Tell me," I demand, narrowing my eyes. "Is it Max?"

"No. Max and I are great. It's…" Her face scrunches as she winces, then takes a deep breath. Apology is written all over her pretty features when she says, "Your parents were asking about you the last time I went home."

Oh.

Little prickles of warning bite at my flesh.

"You saw them?"

"At church."

I exhale a shaky breath, my insides twisting even thinking about them, about Kira talking to them. Almost like it's a betrayal of our friendship, even though I know it's not. I shouldn't be surprised that she spoke with them.

We grew up an hour and a half north of here in a small town, attending the same fundamentalist church. She still goes whenever she's home, which isn't very often, especially since her family found out she was working in a bar. They had a major flip out and practically threatened to disown her if she didn't quit.

That's the type of people the town breeds.

Judgmental.

Critical.

People that shun anyone who disobeys any one of their million rules.

Like me.

Kira got out of there as soon as she had the chance. The day after graduating, she hitched a ride out of town. It was luck, or fate, that she started working in the same small diner that I rented an apartment above.

We reconnected. Our friendship bonded on our rebellion.

I didn't have to tell her all my dirty secrets, because she already knew them – everyone in Springcreek knew.

It's the reason I left at fifteen. Stole a hundred dollars from my dad's underwear drawer and hitchhiked to the first town where I could find a job.

For the first few months, I was afraid that my father

would show up and try to drag me back home. But it soon became obvious that he wasn't looking for me. Nobody was.

"You should go see them," Kira says.

I narrow my eyes at her and say sarcastically, "Right."

"I'm serious. Maybe this is a second chance. Not just for you, but for them, too."

"I'll think about telling them I'm pregnant when you tell your parents you're living with Max."

She snorts. "Point taken. But–"

"I'd rather not talk about them."

"Okay." She smiles sadly, then grabs the remote and turns on the television, flipping through the channels until she finds one of those cheesy made-for-TV movies.

I appreciate the distraction. I know Kira means well, but she doesn't know the whole story. The real reason I ran. I've never told anyone, and I probably never will.

There are some things that are just too dark to share. Some demons that are better left buried in the past.

CHAPTER 15

CARTER

*I*t's hell being away from Layla.

Three weeks, and I feel like another year has passed. But this is the first time I've been able to get away. At least now, hockey is over, and I don't have to go back to New York for two more weeks.

My boss is on me to renew my contract for next season, but I haven't made up my mind, and I won't until I know what I'm going to do about Layla.

If it was up to me, I'd quit my damn job tomorrow, sell my New York apartment, and move in with her permanently. But I'm not sure how well that would go over. Every time I've called over the past few weeks to check in on her, she seemed to have grown more and more withdrawn, like she's purposely distancing herself from me.

I get it. She's scared. And who wouldn't be in her position?

But I need her to realize that I'm not my brother. I won't leave her the second things get hard.

It's past eleven when I pull up to the house in my rental car. The lights inside are off, except a small lamp in the front living room.

I know she's probably already asleep, but the buzz of excitement, just being back in the same house with her, tingles through me. I'm a grown-ass man, but she makes me feel like a goddamn teenager again with his first crush.

The house is quiet when I shut the front door behind me, locking it.

I put my bags down when I see her. Fast asleep on the couch, Layla is curled up, a book lying open on her chest. Her lips are slightly parted, her light brown hair hanging over one soft cheek.

God, she's beautiful, and my fingers itch to touch her.

"Layla?" I take the book and place it on the coffee table, but she doesn't respond.

Her neck is tilted in a funny direction, and I know she's going to be stiff tomorrow if I let her sleep down here.

One arm under her knees, I pick her up, cradling her to my chest.

She stirs slightly, fingers curling into the fabric of my shirt.

"Carter," she mumbles, not opening her eyes.

"I've got you, sweetheart."

She mutters something incoherent, then buries her face against my chest.

My heart does one of those flip flop things, the one that warns me that this thing between us is more than just physical.

Taking my time, because I want to prolong every moment I can while holding her, I carry her up the stairs, glancing once at my bedroom door. For a brief moment, I contemplate taking her in there.

Yeah, that probably wouldn't go over too well.

I sigh and open her door wider with my foot, then gently place her on the bed. But when I try to stand, her fingers continue to grasp my shirt.

"Stay," she murmurs groggily.

I don't know if she's talking in her sleep, or if she actually wants me to stay. The latter makes hope flare in my chest.

"Layla." I place my palm on her cheek.

"Stay," she repeats, her eyes still closed.

How the hell can I argue with that?

I kick off my shoes and crawl in beside her. The second I do, she snuggles close. So close it's like she's using her body as a blanket to cover me. One leg drapes over mine, and her head rests in the crook of my shoulder, her palm flat on my chest.

Her small, curvy little body fits perfectly against mine.

"I'm glad you're back." Her voice is husky with sleep and something more – desire.

She rubs herself against my thigh, and my already hard cock turns to steel.

God, what the woman does to me.

When I shift slightly, she murmurs, "Don't leave."

"I won't." I press my lips against the top of her hair and breathe in her soft, feminine scent.

There's no way in hell I'm leaving.

I also know I won't be getting a minute of sleep tonight. Not when she's wrapped around me, making every damn cell in my body vibrate with need and the ache in my balls grow with every second she's touching me.

But there are some things that are worth the pain – and Layla is definitely one of them.

CHAPTER 16

LAYLA

I wake slowly, my body warm and tingling from the erotic dream I'd been having.

"Carter," I murmur.

His big, strong body is pressed hard against mine, his hands roaming across my skin, touching me in places that beg to be touched.

A small moan escapes my lips, because I don't want to wake up. The dream is too real, and my body hums with pleasure. I can almost feel him beside me, his heavy erection jutting against my backside, his fingers linked with mine.

Suddenly, I'm wide awake, because I realize it isn't just a dream.

Carter is in my bed. His thick, powerful arms are wrapped protectively around me, and yes, his serious morning wood is digging erotically into my back.

Oh. My. God.

My mouth goes dry as I remember bits and pieces of the night before.

Had I actually asked – no begged – him to stay?

I had.

And he did.

Shit. Shit. Shit.

Mortification mixes with arousal.

His breath is warm against my neck, and his cock, hard and heavy, nudges my backside.

I try my best not to move, not to wiggle against him, but it feels so damn good.

It'd be easy to just turn in his arms and let him kiss me. Let him take me. Let him make me feel something other than tainted and used.

Because I know being with Carter would be different. It would be more than just sex.

At least, for me.

He's the one I should have waited for. And I would have. I was going to. I had no intention of messing up my life again because of sex.

But then, there was Travis.

I wasn't a virgin when we slept together, despite how many times he teased me about it.

I'd been with someone years before. But after the firestorm that rained down on me over it, I'd sworn off sex, at least until I found *the one*.

Travis was definitely *not* the one. But he was so damn persistent. And even though he had the whole playboy thing going on, we'd become friends.

And I was lonely.

And drunk.

And he was there.

Just like Carter is now.

A knot forms in my stomach. Is that why I feel the way I

do? Because he's here and I'm lonely?

Mixed emotions swirl through me, fear finally overpowering lust.

I shift away from him, doing my best to untangle myself from his viselike grip.

"Good morning." He stretches, looking just as gorgeous as he always does. He gives me a smile that cuts me to the core, and my stomach flips and twists at what I see in his eyes. Acceptance. Desire. Affection.

I shouldn't let him affect me the way I do. I fight the explosion of emotions that threaten to take me hostage, linking me to this man emotionally, in ways I never thought possible.

It's so easy to freeze up behind my fears, but the way he's watching me, there's that familiar ache I get with him, the one that urges me to just let go.

Sitting up, I self-consciously comb my fingers through my knotted hair.

"Morning," I mutter, fidgeting.

He lifts himself onto his elbows, his smile gone now, and only concern is evident there. Blue eyes, dark and stoic, watch me.

I wish I could do the same, but I'm pretty sure he can read every thought, every emotion, on my face.

"How long are you back for?" I move off the bed and walk to my closet, needing the distance to gather my thoughts.

His gaze is intense when he says, "As long as I need to be."

I don't know what that means. But I'm too damn scared to ask.

Why would he need to be here? For me?

I swallow hard and try to get those damn walls back up, but the way he's watching me, it's like he has the ability to bore through all my defenses with a single look.

"You can do that?" I turn my back to him. "Just work

whenever you want?"

I hear the creak of the bed behind me.

"Hockey season is over. I won't have any work that can't be done from home until September."

"*Home?*" *Is he planning on staying here?*

When he comes up behind me, I turn slightly and look up at him.

"I have an apartment in New York." A muscle in his jaw bunches, and he looks like he's restraining himself from touching me.

If I was smart, I'd take a step away. Instead, I just stand there, silently begging him to pull me into his arms.

He rubs the back of his neck. "But if you want me to stay..."

I swallow hard, not sure what exactly he's asking.

"This is your house. You can stay here whenever you want."

His mouth tightens in a thin line, but he doesn't say anything. He just keeps watching me.

I shift uncomfortably under his gaze. "I need to get ready for work."

"Right." He sighs. "There are some things we should sit down and talk about when you have some time."

A knot forms in my throat.

"Okay," I say, frowning. "Have you heard anything from him? From Travis?"

The muscles in Carter's face tense, and I think I see a flicker of guilt there. "Yeah."

"Oh." Even though I'd asked the question, I hadn't expected that answer. But why should I be surprised that he'd contacted his brother? Of course they still spoke.

"He got a job up north. He..." Carter looks up at the ceiling briefly, the muscle in his jaw pulsating as he glances back at me, his gaze now full of sympathy. "He had some paperwork drawn up by a lawyer. About giving up his paternal rights. He asked me to give it to you."

"Of course." Even though I expected as much from Travis, it still makes my insides twist knowing that he would so easily give up his rights.

"I'm sorry–"

"You need to stop doing that," I snap. "Apologizing. You're not the one I had sex with, and this baby isn't your responsibility."

Carter winces like I've physically slapped him. If my emotions weren't so twisted, and I wasn't so confused, I'd feel bad for my words. But we can't keep walking around pretending that this is anything other than it is.

Sure, it was a bitchy thing to say, especially after how nice he's been to me, but I need those barriers back up, or else I'm in some serious danger of falling for him.

I think he's going to walk out. Actually, I hope that he does. Instead, he just stands there, looking at me with way more compassion than I deserve.

All the pent-up feelings that I've tried to bury inside bubble to the surface, and I can feel my throat tightening. My hands start to shake, and tears blur my vision.

Don't cry, I warn myself, but it's too late.

He takes a step toward me. "Layla–"

"No." I shake my head and put my hands up to stop him from coming closer. One touch and I know I'll lose it completely.

"I'm trying to help."

"If you want to stay here and watch over me, then I can't stop you. But I don't know what you want from me. I can't–" My breath catches on a small sob that I can't hold back.

Carter pulls me against his chest and buries his face in my hair, hushing me like a child that needs comforting.

I want to push him away. I need to push him away. But I

can't. All I can do is melt into his embrace and take all the strength and comfort he's offering.

"I'm..." I gulp in a breath, clutching the hem of his t-shirt in my fists and resting my forehead against his chest. "I'm so confused. I don't know what I'm doing."

"I don't want anything that you're not ready or willing to give." His palms are on my face, fingers tangled in the back of my hair, and he uses his thumbs to force my chin up to look at him. "I'm not pressuring you. I just want to be here. For you. For this baby. That's all."

More tears stream down my cheeks, and my chest tightens. "It's too hard."

"What is?"

"Being with you. Touching you." There's the truth. Right out in the open. And there's no taking it back.

His lips twitch up slightly.

"It's not funny." I frown up at him.

"No. It's not." His grin gets a little bigger, even though I can tell he's trying to hold it back.

I push on his chest, but he doesn't let me go. "Then why are you smiling?"

"Because you want me." He brushes the tears off my cheek with the pad of this thumb and smiles down at me. "I'll let you in on a little secret." He leans down, so that his lips brush against the shell of my ear, and whispers, "I want you, too."

A shiver races across my skin.

I pinch my eyes closed, trying to think of anything other than the way he's holding me, making my body crave him in ways I never thought possible.

"I'm not going to hurt you." His thumb strokes across my bottom lip.

"You don't know that."

"I'm not like my brother. I won't take off the minute it gets hard. I know what I'm getting into."

He doesn't even know the half of it. It's not just this baby or the stuff with Travis. There are things in my past that broke me, and after seven years, I'm not sure I'll ever heal.

Maybe he has some hero complex, wanting to save the damaged and broken damsel in distress.

"I don't need saving, if that's what this is about." I may be damaged, but I don't need a man to make everything better in my life. Even if that man is Carter Bennett.

I put my hands on his chest to push him away, but he captures my wrists.

"That's *not* what this is about." He tilts his head close to mine, his gaze boring into me. "Don't push me away."

Too late. My walls are already up.

"Maybe you've got some white knight complex, but I can take care of myself. I always have."

"Do I look like a white knight, Layla?" His voice is intense, his gaze daring.

I blink up at him. The ink that covers his skin, the dark scruff that shadows his jaw, the piercing blue eyes that scream danger. No, he looks more like the bad boy ready to break my heart than the hero of childhood fantasies. But inside, I know he's more than that. He's good. And honest. And I don't deserve him.

"How can you want this?" I spit out, using my frustration as a weapon against him.

"I want *you*. That's all that matters." The seductive tone of his voice winds through me like liquid heat, warming my blood and sending a thrill racing down my spine, straight to my core.

Unconcealed desire thrums between us with scorching intensity, so strong I can't deny it even if I tried. It's been building since the first night we met. I've tried to push it down. To think that maybe it was just me. Now, he's voiced the truth, and there is no turning back from that.

He wants me. I want him. It's as simple, and as complicated, as that.

Still...

"I don't know." I do know. I want him so bad my body aches with the need to feel him inside me. And more than that, I want his strength, his support – and his love.

Foolishness.

I've never considered myself a weak person. I've been on my own for as long as I can remember, never relying on anyone.

But the promises he's made, and the hope that they fuel. It makes me want. And *wanting* is a very dangerous thing to do.

"You don't have to make any decisions right now." His fingers brush across my face, down my neck. "I'll be patient."

Kiss me, my body screams, despite my mind's protest.

He leans down and I think he's going to. Instead, he presses his lips against my forehead and lets out a small sigh, then pulls back. "I'll go make some coffee."

I'm both grateful and disappointed when he walks out of the room, leaving me alone with my chaotic thoughts.

I want more than anything to trust Carter. To believe that maybe, just maybe, this crazy relationship might work. But there's so much more than just us to think about. There's Travis. And the baby. Not to mention what people would think about me if I just jumped from one brother's bed to the other.

Slut.

Whore.

Those names scream into my brain, condemning me.

I can't do it.

We've already got too many strikes against us.

This thing between us is impossible. Even if he really is *the one*, the world will never accept it.

CHAPTER 17

LAYLA

*C*arter is true to his word. He's more than patient. I know now why Travis nicknamed him *Saint fucking Carter*. The man truly has the tolerance of a saint. Even during my emotional outbursts and crying spells, which have become more and more regular lately – damn those pregnancy hormones! – he just holds me and reassures me that everything is going to be all right. He's convincing enough that I'm actually starting to believe it.

As the days and weeks go by with him living under the same roof, it starts to become easy to accept him in my life, mostly because he's always here.

And it's nice – more than nice. It's wonderful.

When I wake up in the morning, there's a pot of decaf coffee waiting for me, and when I get home from work, he usually has dinner waiting for me. I've stopped trying to avoid him by staying in my room in the evenings. Instead, I join him in the living room and curl up on the couch beside him, reading a book while he watches whatever game is on television.

He hasn't tried anything with me, and I haven't asked him back into my room, but that doesn't mean the connection isn't there. If anything, it's just continued to grow stronger. Only now, I'm starting to realize that my bad boy hero who saved me from being run over by a car a little over a year ago isn't really so bad – he's actually really sweet.

But he's also the most stubborn, pig-headed man I've ever met. I know he'd say the same thing about me, but the difference is *I'm right*. At least, when it comes to my work. We've had more than a few arguments over how often I'm on my feet. But so far, I've won every single one. Because not all of us can be former NHL stars that can work if and when they want.

But I don't begrudge him for it. I know he worked his ass off getting where he did, and even now, he constantly stays busy.

I came home from work early last week to find him in the basement with a construction crew, working alongside them on whatever project he has going on down there.

And he cleans.

He's meticulous with everything. I thought I was a neat freak, but he's worse. When Travis lived here, I was constantly cleaning up after him and his friends. But Carter has respected my space, only once bringing a friend back to the house, and then only for dinner and a few beers on the back porch.

The guy really is perfect. And I kind of hate him for it. Because it makes the temptation that much worse.

We've become…friends. And that's something.

No, it's not ideal, and yes, it's still complicated, but it's nice to have someone other than Kira to talk to.

It's nice to not be alone.

Carter is sitting on the couch, crouched over his laptop that sits on the coffee table, brows drawn down as he types furiously.

Every time I see him, I can't help the butterflies that flutter in my chest. No amount of time will ever dull how freaking gorgeous the man is. His hair is long right now, needing a trim and hanging over his eyes. And the dark scruff has grown into a decent beard that he keeps neatly trimmed. I've never been a fan of beards, but on him it just looks sexy and rugged. With that, combined with the ink that covers his bulging biceps and forearms, he oozes primal sexiness.

Get a grip, Layla. I blink away the thought.

"I'll stop by the grocery store after work. Do you need anything?"

"You're working again?" Carter looks up from his computer and frowns at me. There it is. The dark, broody look he gets when he disproves of something I do.

"I'm taking an extra shift at the restaurant this week," I say evenly, giving him my own look that says not to argue with me.

"If you need money–"

"We've talked about this."

"I know." He shuts his laptop and stands.

Shit. Here we go. While I appreciate his concern, I can't let him think that I need to be taken care of, especially not financially. Letting me live here for practically nothing is already more than enough.

I search my purse for my keys, and a lip gloss falls out of one pocket onto the floor. I lean over to pick it up, but when I straighten up, my vision starts to darken to a single point of light in front of me.

Crap.

I drop my purse, reaching frantically for the wall, or anything to stop myself from passing out.

"Damn it, Layla." Carter's voice is too far away, and I know there's no way he'll get to me in time.

I'm falling fast.

My body hits something hard and warm, and it takes me a second to realize it's Carter. Next thing I know, my feet are no longer on the floor and he has me cradled against his chest.

"Put me down." I squirm in his arms as my vision returns.

"I'm taking you to the hospital."

"It was just a dizzy spell. It's normal. I've already talked to my doctor about it."

"That's the second time you've passed out in my arms. There's nothing normal about it."

"I have to go to work." I wriggle against him, but he's too damn strong. "Put. Me. Down."

"No," he growls, and his blue eyes are dark and possessive when he looks down at me. "Not until I know you're all right."

"I'm fine." I go limp, knowing there's no sense fighting. I'm pretty sure he'll toss me over his shoulder like a goddamn caveman and carry me to the hospital if he has to.

"I'd rather have a doctor's opinion."

"I'm not going to the damn doctor because I was a little dizzy."

"Well, you're not going to work, either." He puts me on the couch. When I start to move, he points a finger and snarls, "Stay."

As sexy as the whole Neanderthal, possessive thing is, I really can't deal with this today. Twice last week I was late because my stomach wouldn't settle, and the week before that I missed an entire shift because I was so sick I couldn't get out of bed.

"Here." He hands me a glass of water, then moves my hair off my neck and places a cool washcloth on it.

How the hell am I supposed to stay mad at him when he does stuff like that? Why can't he be an insufferable jerk like every other guy I've known?

I take a sip, more to appease him than anything, and then place the glass on the side table. "You don't have to worry about me."

"Someone does. You're pushing yourself too hard when you don't have to."

"Yes. I do." I start to stand and regret it immediately. The room spins and I have to sit down again.

"That's it. I'm taking you in." The growl in his voice makes me not argue, because I've gotten to know his moods pretty well, and there's no arguing with the one he's in now.

Yeah, stubborn doesn't even begin to describe Carter Bennett.

Thirty minutes later, we're in the small exam room of my family doctor's office. I'm pretty sure her schedule was completely booked, but Carter was more than a little insistent, and the meek-looking woman behind the desk looked both terrified and enamored by him – a common reaction to the mammoth-sized man.

Now, he's pacing the small room, his arms crossed over his chest, a deep frown on his face.

"Would you stop that?" I'm sitting on the exam table wearing one of those ridiculous paper gowns. "Or I'm kicking you out."

I didn't want him coming in to begin with, but it was another of his absurd demands.

"I want to hear what the doctor has to say."

"You don't trust me?"

He grunts, leaning against the counter, his muscular arms crossed over his chest.

The door opens then, and Dr. Evans comes in, her silvery gaze going straight to Carter. The woman has to be in her late sixties, but I can see her appreciative look as she takes him in. Another common reaction.

She holds out her hand to him. "You must be the father. It's nice to finally meet you."

Heat slams into my face and my mouth goes dry.

"Nice to meet you, too." His face remains stoic as he shakes her hand, but I don't miss the flicker of emotion in his eyes.

Dr. Evans turns to me and smiles. "What brings you in today?"

"She fainted. Twice," Carter says, all growly and possessive.

I glare over at him before looking back at the doctor. "I've had a few dizzy spells, that's all."

"She practically collapsed in my arms this morning." He looks at me as if daring me to argue with him.

I shake my head. "I'm fine. Really."

"We'll check your blood pressure, and I'll order a few tests." She places the cuff around my arm and smiles up at Carter as if she's falling for his grizzly bear act. "Have you heard the baby's heartbeat yet?"

"No," we say in unison.

It had been too early the last time I'd been in.

She places her stethoscope on my arm, watching the numbers on the machine, then uncuffs me. "Your blood pressure is a bit low, but nothing concerning. Just try not to stand up too quickly."

"See," I say to Carter.

He keeps frowning, not looking convinced.

The doctor places a blanket over my legs, then lifts the gown, exposing the slight, almost imperceptible rounding of my belly.

She squirts jelly on my stomach and I flinch at the coldness. The minute she presses the microphone-looking device against my skin, the room fills with a soft thumping.

"There it is." Dr. Evans smiles at both of us. "Nice and strong."

Oh, wow.

My baby's heartbeat.

Tears prick in my eyes, but I don't even try to brush them away when they start to slip down my cheek.

Carter reaches for my hand, and his big strong fingers wrap around mine. When I look up at him, I see emotion reflected in his gaze. He gives me a small smile.

The doctor is saying something, but I barely hear her words. All I can focus on is the sound of my baby's heartbeat, and the way Carter is watching me now.

"…and try to rest whenever you can."

I do catch her last words, mostly because of Carter's reaction.

His head snaps up. "I'll make sure of it."

I can't help but roll my eyes, wanting to slap the doctor for giving him even a small excuse to lock me up in the house.

"We'll see you both in a few more weeks for your scheduled ultrasound."

Carter helps me sit up when we're alone again.

"I told you everything is fine," I mumble.

"She said you need to rest more."

Of course, *that's* what he picked up on.

He hands me my clothes, and stands there, watching me.

"Can you turn around?"

He grunts, but turns slightly.

I pull my jeans on, and have to suck in a breath to do the button up. Another reminder that I'm going to need to buy maternity clothes soon. Another expense that I can barely afford. This is why I *need* to work.

"Can you drop me off at the diner on the way home?"

"I already called and told them you wouldn't be in today."

"You did what?"

He turns to look at me, but I'm still naked from the top up.

"Turn around." I grab my shirt to cover myself, heat warming my cheeks.

His eyes darken, and it takes him a second longer than it should to redirect his gaze.

When his back is to me again, I ball my fingers into fists, take a couple deep breaths, and try not to completely lose it on him. But he makes it so damn easy.

"You shouldn't have done that without asking me. I told you I need the money."

"No, you don't. I'll help you with whatever you need."

"I'm not going to be a charity case." I shove my head and arms through my shirt and adjust it.

"Me wanting to take care of you doesn't make you a charity case."

"Then what does it make me? 'Cause I can think of a lot worse words."

He turns then, fire in his eyes. "It makes you *mine.*"

Oh.

Silence.

He takes a step towards me, and I know I should back away. But my legs lock, and my heart starts to pound frantically in my chest.

"It makes you mine, Layla," he repeats, reaching out and placing his palm on my cheek.

I can tell he's holding back, seeing his control starting to fray. There's hunger in his eyes, sexual and intense.

Either I run now, or I give in.

This is the crux.

The point of no return.

He dips his head, his blue gaze intense and unyielding. His mouth is so close to mine. Just a breath away. I can practically taste his kiss.

And God, he smells so good.

"I'll wait for however long you need. But I'm not going to pretend that it's not killing me not being able to touch you." His head dips closer, his thumb stroking my face. "All you have to do is say yes, sweetheart."

"I…" Am so freaking scared.

"Say yes, Layla." It's more of a demand than a request.

My mouth parts. I'm willing myself to say no, but the word doesn't come out, just a shaky breath.

Yes. Yes. Yes.

I want him.

Bad.

And right now, staring into his intense blue eyes, I can't remember a single reason why I've resisted for so long.

I give a small nod, and it's enough of an answer for him because, the next thing I know, his mouth crashes down on mine, consuming me, tasting me, pushing me over an invisible edge where control and reservations are lost.

His hands are tangled in my hair, and his hard body presses against mine, his mouth and tongue teasing mine, spurring my own wild desire.

A small whimper escapes my lips and he growls, deepening the kiss.

Fire. It burns through me. My skin is alight with it.

It's more than just a kiss. He's marking me, claiming me.

My palms are on his chest, and I feel the raging beat of his heart, proof that he's just as aroused as I am.

His hold is possessive, his kiss merciless.

"My God, Layla. What you do to me." His tongue sweeps over my swollen lips.

He pulls back, his breathing ragged, nostrils flaring, and a primal hunger burning in his eyes.

"Let's go." His voice drops an octave. One large hand wraps around my waist, guiding me out of the room, through the building, and towards the parking lot.

He's silent all the way to the car, but his hands are on me, possessive and tight. The look on his face is unreadable. I swear, he'd toss me over his shoulder and carry me to the car if there weren't a handful of people watching.

I have no idea what he's thinking, or why he's gone all dark and broody.

When he opens the car door for me, I blink up at him. "Carter–"

"Get in the car, Layla." His voice rumbles through me.

"Where are we going?"

"Home." His hands rest on the hood of the car, trapping me as he leans in and whispers in my ear, his voice rough and dripping with need. "Our home. And I'm going to show you just how *mine* you really are."

CHAPTER 18

CARTER

*L*ayla is quiet the entire drive back to the house. She keeps glancing at me from the corner of her eyes, like she's expecting me to pull over at any moment and rip her clothes off.

I'll admit, the thought crossed my mind. It took all my restraint not to take her in the goddamn exam room.

That small nod. It's all the confirmation I needed. She may not know exactly what she agreed to, but I plan to show her – today.

She's afraid of me. I can see it in her eyes. Maybe not of me, but of the way I make her feel. Of what I'm offering her.

There are a lot of things I've learned about her over the past few weeks, and one of them is that she doesn't believe she deserves to be happy. That much is obvious. But I'm going to show her differently. Make her see how fucking special she really is.

She's fidgeting, her fingers nervously picking at some

imaginary spot on her shirt. I take her hand, wrapping my own much larger one around it, and hold it tight until we pull into the driveway.

I hear her swallow hard, and feel her body tremble as her gaze goes toward the house.

"You have nothing to be afraid of, sweetheart." I squeeze her hand once before releasing it and getting out of the car.

It takes her a few seconds before she follows my lead.

There's so much hesitancy in her expression now, and when I shut the front door, I know that if I don't make a move, she's going to run.

And we'll be taking three steps backward.

Not happening.

"Come here." I take her hand, pulling her towards me. I wrap one arm around her, my other hand cradling the back of her head.

She chews on her bottom lip, her gaze trained on my chest, brows drawn down.

"Look at me, Layla." I move my hand down, placing my palm on her lower back, and slowly her eyes raise to meet mine. That's better. Soft brown eyes blink up at me.

Yes, there's fear, but there's also need reflected there.

And trust.

The one thing I've been waiting for.

I stroke my knuckles across her cheek, down her neck and across her collarbone, feeling her tremble and watching her eyes close slightly. Her lips part in an inaudible sigh.

Awareness speaks between us, making me feel things I know I've never felt before.

My God, she completely undoes me.

"So beautiful," I whisper, leaning down and lightly brushing my lips against hers. "I want to touch you. Every part of you. I want my mouth on yours. On your skin..." Nipping gently at her ear, I growl, "On your body."

The sound, half-moan and half-whimper, that vibrates in her throat has my balls rock hard against my body. There won't be a part of her that I don't own when I'm finished.

"Carter," she murmurs, melting against me.

My entire body is tight, and the frenzied need to pull my cock out and take her hard and fast right here in the damn foyer is overwhelming. I can't help the feral groan that escapes my lips. Hearing her say my name, the way it's almost a plea, does all sorts of things to me.

"I want you."

I almost lose it completely with her admission.

Leaning down, I scoop her up in my arms, and she lets out a small squeal.

"Bed," I growl out, starting up the stairs, two at a time. "Now."

Her lips twitch up, and I can almost feel the laugh she's holding in.

"What?" I kick my bedroom door open with my foot, shutting it behind me.

"You're just all…" She licks her lips and runs her fingers across the scruff on my cheek.

It's one of the first caresses she's initiated, and it does something to me.

"All what?" I demand, placing her on the bed and hovering over her, palms flat on either side of her head.

"Alpha male."

I chuckle. "You have no idea, sweetheart."

"Then show me." Her fingers tug at the hem of my shirt, then slip beneath, trailing up my abs and chest.

This time, I can't control the growl that leaves my throat.

God, I want to sink straight into her.

I reach back and pull my shirt over my head, tossing it to the floor while she tugs at my belt. When her fingers start for the zipper, I grip her wrists. "Slow down, love. As much as I want to devour you right now, I also want to take my time. Memorize every inch of you."

"Your words," she says against my lips when I kiss her again. "How am I supposed to resist you?"

"You're not." I kiss her hard once more before pulling back and kneeling on the bed. I take her wrists and pull her up so that she's mirroring me, and place her hands on my chest, on the ink that she's always stealing glances at when she thinks I'm not looking.

Her gaze skims the patterns, then her fingers begin tracing the designs, and a small smile tugs at her lips, her eyes filled with appreciation.

"They're beautiful," she says softly, her touch sending heat burning through my body.

My fingers skim under her shirt, cupping one breast over the fabric of her lacy bra. "*You're* beautiful."

She moans, and my mouth crashes down on hers once more. Her arms wrap around my neck, fingers burying in my hair. Needing to remove the barriers between us, I pull her shirt off, then unclasp the back of her bra, discarding them quickly before starting on the button of her pants.

"Lie down," I demand, pushing her back against the bed. I slide my fingers under the material, hooking my thumb on her panties, then drag my hands down her legs, removing the remaining obstructions.

Pushing her knees apart with my own, I kneel above her, taking in her perfection.

She watches me, wariness returning with self-consciousness.

"Do you have any idea how gorgeous you are?" I ask, taking one breast in my palm and the other in my mouth, the nipples pebbling against my touch.

"You make me feel beautiful." Her back arches to receive my touch, her legs relaxing and opening wider so that I can feel the warmth of her pussy against my chest. She wiggles beneath me, her body demanding more.

Holy hell, she makes me crazy with lust.

Those breasts, those curves, and that soft milky skin. She's more than beautiful, she's a fucking goddess.

I drag my hand down the soft curve of her stomach, resting there for moment, with the reminder of the child she's carrying.

My child. No, it may not be mine biologically, but I'll be the one who raises it. And if I get my way, which I will, I'll be the one it calls Daddy.

Shifting between her legs, I press my lips where my hand had been moments before and feel her still, her muscles tightening slightly.

"Mine," I growl against her stomach, watching her eyes widen slightly. I see the small flicker of hope there. "Both of you."

She bites down on her lip and gives a small nod, and my chest swells.

This is what I want. What I've been longing for. I clench my jaw, a deep sound of pleasure leaving me.

Trailing a kiss downward, I stroke the inside of her thigh until she opens wider for me, letting me trail my tongue across the slit of her pussy.

She moans, twisting, and lifts her hips towards my touch. I slip one finger in and she gasps, then lets out a sound of pleasure when I find her sensitive nub with my mouth, flicking my tongue over it and making her squirm even more.

Sliding one more finger inside her, I feel her walls clench around me. She's so damn tight and wet. My cock is pulsating against the rough fabric of my pants, demanding entrance.

Patience, I remind myself, wanting to prolong every moment of pleasure.

She's responsive to every touch, every lick, every flick of my tongue, and it isn't long before her body starts to quiver and pulsate with her growing orgasm.

"That's it, sweetheart. Come for me," I murmur against her pussy, two fingers thrusting inside her, my other hand teasing one of her hard nipples.

"Carter. Oh my God." Her hands fist in my hair, and she cries out as her body convulses, her tight walls clenching and spasming around my fingers.

My God, is right. I haven't even been inside of her, and I'm already addicted.

I kiss her once more on the inside of her thigh, then crawl above her and grin. "I've been fantasizing about doing that for far too long."

She blushes. "No one has ever done *that* before."

I try not to frown at her admission, but it unsettles me. Obviously, she's not a virgin, but it makes me wonder how innocent she really is.

"Did I say something wrong?" she asks, concern drawing her brows down.

"No." I kiss her forehead, her nose, then her lips. "Of course not."

"I just want to be gentle with you."

She tugs my hair then, pulling me down towards her in a demanding kiss.

I groan at the next words that come out of her mouth. "I don't want gentle. I just want you. All of you."

CHAPTER 19

LAYLA

My body is still humming from his touch, but I want so much more. I know he's holding back, but I don't want his control. I want—no, I need—all that intense, dark hunger that's been building between us to finally explode.

He's watching me, fire in his gaze, and I can practically see the war that's going on inside of him. The man struggles with the beast within.

"Please," I beg, my hands travelling down his sculpted abs to the waist of his pants, hooking my fingers in the material and pushing it over his hips. "I need you."

The truth of my words leaves me shaking. I do need him. More than I've ever allowed myself to need anyone.

I swallow hard when his cock springs free, my mouth watering for a taste. I lick my lips and he groans.

"There's no way in hell I'm going to last if you put those sweet lips around me," he growls out.

I give a small pout, and he chuckles.

"There'll be lots of time for that in the future, but I've been waiting too damn long to be inside of you. I'm already barely hanging onto my control."

That makes me smile. I love that I can do that to him. Make him want me with that much need.

I reach out and stroke his long length, reveling in the silkiness of it.

"I don't have anything." He moves above me, pressing his cock against my stomach, his thick thighs spreading my legs wider.

It takes a second for me to realize that he means protection.

"I'm clean," I whisper against his lips as he kisses me.

"So am I," he says, the restraint in his voice fraying.

I place my palms on his face and lock my gaze with his, my heart hammering in my chest. "Then make love to me."

Maybe it's not the right thing to say. Maybe I should have told him to just take me, or have sex with me. But this thing between us is so much more than that. At least, I think it is. Maybe I just want it to be.

The intensity in his gaze as he moves above me, pressing the head of his heavy erection at my entrance, is almost too much.

I gasp as his hips thrust forward, and he buries himself deep inside of me.

"God, Layla," he breathes out, resting his forehead against mine and giving me a moment for my body to adjust to his width and length.

There's a delicious ache between my legs as my walls tighten and relax. My experience with sex is limited to a couple drunken encounters, and this is more than I've ever experienced.

The realness of it. His body connected to mine. I'm aware of his every slight movement, every breath, every heartbeat.

I love you, I want to cry out as he starts to move inside of me. Instead, I hold onto him, shutting off my brain, and trying to shut off my emotions.

An impossible task. Because already, I'm in way over my head, and I know that after tonight, after this, losing him won't just break me, it'll destroy me.

His hands are all over me now, stroking down my thigh, across my breasts, his thumb playing with my nipple and causing more sensations to pulsate straight to my core.

I close my eyes, unable to look at his beautiful face. Not when my body is singing with pleasure, and he's pushing me to places I've never been before. My legs wrap around his hips, my fingers dig into his back, and I move with him, each thrust, each stroke more demanding than the last.

"Eyes"–He thrusts deep–"On"–And his palm is on my face–"Me."

I blink up at him as he rides me harder, my body overloaded with sensations, my emotions twisting this incredible experience into something more than I know it is.

I can feel my orgasm building, and can sense his, too. So close.

"Let go, sweetheart." His intense blue gaze bores into me, demanding more than just my body.

His hips buck against mine, his body filling and stretching me, making it impossible to resist the pleasure that all but consumes me.

I feel myself giving in, because I don't have the strength to fight it.

"Carter," I whimper against his lips as his mouth crashes against mine. My fingers tangle in his hair and I try to breathe in a ragged breath, but I can't get enough oxygen into my system. It's like I'm being tortured with pleasure, and I don't know if I'll survive.

His quick, hard strokes have me exploding in seconds. A flood of sensation wracks my body and every muscle tenses and tightens. I cry out. What, I don't know. All I know is that for a moment, I swear I lose consciousness as the orgasm that was building rips almost violently through my entire body.

Pure, blissful rapture. Wave after wave of pleasure rolls through me.

In some distant place, I hear Carter's own cry of release, and feel his body contract and explode within me. I feel his seed spill with a force that drives me even further over the edge.

When the last shudder rips through me, I cling to him, trembling with how completely and utterly spent I am. Physically and emotionally.

Carter rests his forehead against mine, and his fingers brush across my damp cheeks.

"What's wrong?" He shifts up on one arm, still not pulling out of me, brows drawn down in a frown.

I realize then that the dampness is tears.

No. No. No.

I am not crying. Not after how perfect everything was.

"I-I'm okay." But my voice betrays my emotions.

"Did I hurt you?" He starts to ease away, and I panic, gripping his hips and forcing him not to move.

"No. You were…that was perfect."

His knuckles drag across my cheek, and he presses a light kiss against my lips. "Talk to me, sweetheart."

The way he's looking at me, like I'm the most precious thing in the world, makes me feel safe. Like maybe this whole insane thing between us might just be the real thing. That I might not be the fool I think I am for falling head over heels for the guy.

I trace one of the patterns on his bicep and think about what I'm supposed to say. I've never been here before, in a place where the guy wants me to open up. I've spent my whole life bottling my emotions. I don't know how to let my walls down completely.

When I don't answer, Carter rolls over on his back, taking me with him, so that my head is resting on his chest and one of his arms is wrapped possessively around me.

We lay in silence for a long time, and I swear I fall even more in love with him, for his ability to know exactly what I need. And right now, I just need time to think.

My mind never stops. It's constantly thinking about the consequences of every word I say, every small, insignificant action, and this…well, this is going to take a hell of a lot of processing.

"I'm scared," I say, being brutally honest. "If this doesn't work out between us…" My breath hitches, and I pinch my eyes shut. "I'll survive. I know I will. But I don't know what…"

More tears stream down my cheeks, and I hate it. I've always been able to hide my emotions, to rein back my tears. But with him, I can't.

His thumb is under my chin, tilting my face up to meet his gaze.

"You're mine now, Layla. Do you know what that means?" His expression is dark, confident. "It means I'm not letting you go. Ever."

I let out an uneven breath. I want that. More than anything. But words fail me.

Is it possible? Him and me? Can we live this life? Despite everything?

He fills places in me that I didn't even know were empty.

I don't want to let that go.

I don't want to let *him* go.

I just pray that when everything is said and done, I won't have to.

CHAPTER 20

CARTER

"*W*hat's this?" Layla frowns at the large bag I place on the kitchen table in front of her. When she stands, she places one hand on her growing belly, and the other on her lower back, stretching.

It's been almost two months since she finally said yes to me. I don't even know if she realizes it, but we've started to create a home together. I've even convinced her to move her stuff into my room so that we can start turning hers into a nursery.

Those damn walls of hers are still up, and I want more than she's ready to give me. But for now, what we're doing is working.

"It's a gift," I say, moving around the table to kiss her. Open it."

Biting her bottom lip, she pulls the box out of the bag and gasps.

"It's a MacBook Pro." I wrap my arms around her so that her back is against my chest, and I nuzzle my nose in her hair, breathing in her sweet scent. "I thought you could use an upgrade on the dinosaur that you have."

"I can't accept this." She puts the box back on the table. "It's worth more than I make in an entire month."

A part of me wants to correct her. It's worth more than she *did* make in a month. I've finally convinced her to take a leave from both jobs. Her only condition was that she still volunteer at the animal shelter each week.

"Now that you have some free time, I thought you might like to write some more. You can barely get on the Internet with that old thing."

"I told you, I'm not writing anymore." She frowns, looking away.

"That was before."

"Before what?"

I grip her chin and plant a hard kiss on her lips, then pull back with a smirk "Before me."

She laughs and shakes her head.

"I think I've given you some new writing material." I wink, and tap her nose playfully.

"You have." Her lips twitch up, her eyes sparkling.

I love that smile. The one when she allows herself a moment to set aside her fear. It doesn't happen very often, but when it does, it does something inside of me.

"I can give you a few more things to write about right now." I pull her against my chest and rake my teeth across the soft skin below her ear. I feel her tremble.

Being with Layla, spending time with her, is the best thing in the world. But God, the sex – it's beyond anything I've ever experienced. Maybe because my emotions are involved. I don't know. I just know that every time we make love, it's like the first time. Pure, erotic pleasure, mixed with raw emotions. The combination is untainted rapture.

"You're changing the subject." Her voice is a half whimper as my hands and mouth stroke across her sensitive skin.

"Maybe," I smile. "But I have something else to show you."

Another frown tugs at her lips. She hates gifts and surprises, but I'm praying she'll love this one.

"What is it?" Her eyes narrow suspiciously.

"Come on and I'll show you." I take her hand, pulling her to the back stairwell that leads to the basement. I open the door.

"You're finally going to let me see your new man cave?"

I chuckle at the small lie I'd told her to keep her away from the construction. "Close your eyes."

"I'm not going to close my eyes and walk down the stairs."

"And I'm not going to let you fall. Now, close your damn eyes."

She sighs like I've just asked her to clean the toilets, or something equally as terrible, but finally submits.

"Keep them closed," I warn, taking her elbows and leading her down, past the laundry room, and opening the double barn-style doors that lead to the main living area.

Flicking on the lights, I inhale my own shaky breath and drag my fingers through my hair, hoping to hell that she's not going to be pissed about this.

"Well?" she asks, eyes still closed.

"Okay. Open them."

She blinks, once, twice, then her eyes widen as she takes in the room. The full oak bookshelves that line every wall, the extra wide armchair that sits in the corner, and the antique desk with its ergonomic leather chair.

"It's a library, or an office. Whatever you want it to be," I say, watching her as she slowly starts to walk around the room, fingers brushing the spines of the books. "I thought you'd like to have your own space. Somewhere for you to read, or write, or whatever you want to do. The computer is only the finishing touch."

She turns and blinks at me, brows drawn down. "You did all this? For me?"

There it is, the look that says she doesn't think she deserves it.

I remove the distance between us and place my hands on her shoulders. "Yes. And this isn't something I can take back, so don't even think about arguing with me."

She laughs, but there are tears in her eyes.

"Do you like it? I had an interior decorator choose the color, but if you–"

"It's perfect." Her arms lift, wrapping around my neck, and she stands on her toes to kiss me. "Thank you," she says against my lips. "No one has ever done anything like this for me. I love it."

Thank God. I breathe out a heavy sigh of relief.

She kisses me again, this time harder and longer, and her hands skim down my chest and snake under my shirt.

"I thought you had to volunteer today." I chuckle, seeing the intent in her eyes.

"I can be a few minutes late." She grins up at me, her touch instantly making me hard.

We both frown when the doorbell rings.

"Are you expecting anyone?"

She shakes her head.

"Okay, I'll get it."

"Carter?" she says, stopping me before I can make it through the double doors. "Thank you."

I smile, my heart swelling, knowing the fact that she accepted it is a huge step. The doorbell rings a few more times in an impatient manner. I grumble and make my way up the stairs, ready to give whoever's on the other side of the door an earful.

"Kira?" I frown when I take in the woman's worried, almost frenzied appearance. "Is everything all right?"

"Is Layla here?" she asks, stepping into the house when I open the door wider.

"She's downstairs. I'll get her." A weird feeling settles in the pit of my stomach when I call down for Layla to come up. It's like that moment before something bad happens. You know it's coming, but there's nothing you can do to stop it.

I just hope I'm wrong.

"What's wrong?" Layla must feel it, too, because her face pales, and that fear that's almost constantly in her eyes—that had been dissipating these past couple months—is back, full force.

"You weren't answering your phone. I've been trying to call you for the last hour," Kira says, shuffling from one foot to the other.

"It must be turned off. Are you okay? Is it Max?"

I'm assuming Max is the boyfriend I still haven't met.

"No." Kira shakes her head. "I'm sorry, Layla."

Layla doesn't move, not even a fraction of an inch, but I can almost see her starting to shut down.

"It's your mom." Kira looks at me, then back at Layla. "She had a stroke. She's alive, but it's…really bad."

A small, sharp breath is her only reaction. I'm behind her now, hands on her shoulders, but she doesn't lean back against me like she normally does. She just holds herself stiffly, her uneven breathing the only indication that she's upset.

"When?"

"Two days ago. I'm sorry. I just found out. She's at University Hospital in Rosedale."

"Come on. I'll drive."

119

Layla shakes her head, staring vacantly at a spot on the wall. "I can't go."

"It's your mom," Kira says. "Whatever differences you had, they don't matter right now."

Something passes between them that I don't understand. A look that speaks of secrets and regrets.

There's still so much I don't know about her, or about her family. Why she never sees them, or anyone other than Kira, for that matter.

It's like she's all alone in the world. Lost. Afraid. And I want to know why.

"Kira's right." I cup Layla's face in my hands, and she blinks back tears when she looks up at me.

"You don't understand." Her gaze is on the floor, on anything but me.

"You're right. I don't know what happened between you two. But I do know you'll regret not seeing her if she doesn't make it through this."

Silence stretches between us.

"Your mom would want to see you," Kira finally says. "I can come–"

"No." Closing her eyes, Layla rubs her temples.

"I'll take you." I brush her hair away from her cheek. "I promise I won't leave your side. When my parents died, I'd been in an argument with my dad. It destroyed me that the last words I had with him were spoken out of anger."

"The difference is your parents loved you, and I'm sure they knew how much you loved them."

"All parents love their children. Some just have a more difficult time showing it."

She chuckles darkly, the sound sending a chill down my spine.

"All right. I'll go if you really think I should."

I kiss her forehead. "I do."

She gives me a small nod, but when I see the panic and shame clouding her eyes as she starts towards the door, I wonder if I made the right decision convincing her to go.

CHAPTER 21

LAYLA

*M*y entire body is shaking as we take the elevator up to the fifth floor. Not the small trembles that I feel when Carter touches me, but full-out shakes that I can't control. I ball my fingers into fists, biting the inside of my cheek hard. I try to make it less noticeable, but I'm pretty sure everyone, including Carter, can see my fear.

I hate that after all these years, my parents can still do that to me. Turn me into a frightened child.

"It'll be all right." Carter's arm is around my shoulders, steadying me.

I know it's a bad idea bringing him here, but I've never needed him more than I do right now.

"Susan Harper's room?" Carter asks the nurse at the counter.

She looks at her charts, then says, "Second door on the right."

I'm not sure how my feet keep moving, but they do.

It's been seven years since I've seen my parents. No calls. No letters. Even after they knew where I was, they never tried to contact me.

And I'm not sure how they're going to respond to seeing me now. That's if my mom is even conscious enough to know who I am. From the way Kira made it sound, she doesn't have long.

As frightened as I am, I'm glad that Carter convinced me to come. I've never stopped missing my mom. And he's right, I'd be devastated if I never got the chance to say goodbye.

But then, what if they don't want me here? My dad is a big man. Not as big as Carter, but he carries himself with all the self-righteousness and arrogance of a man who puts himself far above others.

I doubt that's changed. And if it hasn't, who knows what kind of scene he'll make. Or what he'll say.

"I shouldn't be here." I stop outside the room the nurse said was my mom's, coldness seeping through my veins.

"I'll be right by your side." His hand takes mine and he gives it a small reassuring squeeze.

With a heavy breath, I push open the door.

It's a single room, one bed, and at first I think the nurse must have given us the wrong room, because I barely recognize the woman in the bed.

Her hair, once a light ashy brown, is now almost pure silver. And there are deep lines in her face that weren't there before. Tubes and wires are everywhere. In her nose, her throat, her arm. But what really distorts her features is that one side of her face looks off, almost slack, giving her an asymmetrical appearance.

This isn't my mom. It can't be.

A shiver races down my spine as I stare at her, unable to move forward.

The woman I knew was strong. Stern. Unbending. But the one in the bed is weak, fragile, a shadow of who she once was.

I swallow hard, wanting to turn and run out of the room. But Carter is behind me, his hand pressed on my back, giving me the strength to move forward.

"Mom?" Blinking back tears, I take a few steps and stand beside the bed. With her frail hand in mine, I say, "Mom. It's me. Layla."

Her skin is so pale it's almost transparent, her veins blue and exposed.

I can't help the tears that start to roll down my cheeks. Seven years of built-up regret, anger, and grief rush through me in a tidal wave of emotions.

"I'm so sorry." The words come out in a sob.

Her eyes, or rather her eye, because the other one doesn't seem to be working properly, flutters open.

There's recognition there. I see it in her expression. And she squeezes my hand, so faint it's barely noticeable. But I notice, and it gives me a small sliver of hope.

"Hi, Mom," I croak out, my voice shaky.

Through the tubes in her throat, she tries to say something.

"Don't try to speak." I kiss her forehead, still holding her hand, and choke back a sob. "I've missed you so much. I'm so sorry. For everything."

A single tear slides down her cheek, and I wipe it away for her.

"I love you."

She blinks three times. I don't know if it's meant to mean anything, but I take it as her saying those words back to me. Words that she barely ever said when I was younger.

It was good to come. My chest swells, because I don't see

any of the anger or animosity that had been in her eyes the last time we'd been together. All I see is love reflected there.

"I'm sorry I didn't come to visit sooner–"

"What is this?" A deep baritone voice laced with loathing rumbles through the small room.

Dread trickles down my spine.

Carter immediately goes into fight mode. I see it in his stance. "She's just visiting. We don't want any trouble–"

"Trouble?" he barks. "That's all that girl is. Trouble."

Knowing the special moment is over, I place my mom's hand back on the bed and turn to meet my father's glare with one of my own.

His face is red, lips drawn up in a scowl. When his eyes drop to the barely concealed rounding of my stomach, a look of pure disgust washes over his features.

"You taint your mother's deathbed with your presence. Get out of here!"

"I came to–"

"I said, get out of here. Now." He takes a step forward and looks like he's about to physically remove me if I don't do what he says, but Carter steps in front of him, shielding me.

The monitors that are hooked up to my mom start to beep faster.

"Can't you see you're upsetting her by being here." He pushes past us, then walks around the bed and takes my mother's hand.

"Sir," Carter says, his frustration barely contained. "We're not here to cause trouble. Layla only wanted to see her mother. You can understand that."

"Dad, please."

"Do *not* call me that. I'm not your father. You're nothing to me. Just a little whore who can't keep her legs closed."

"You have no right to speak to her like that." For a second,

I think Carter might hit him. His fingers are tight fists, and his nostrils flare, his breathing ragged.

"And you." He looks at Carter, and I can see him taking in the tattoos, his scruff, and the way he's dressed. "You're the heathen that got her knocked up again?"

Carter's brows go down as he processes my father's words. Or rather the one word – *again*.

I want to cry. To run. To lock myself in a room and never come out. First, I need to get away from here.

"Carter." I place a hand on his arm. "Let's go."

He continues to glower at my father, like he's still debating whether to take a shot at him. They stare at each other for a long, tense moment, until the door opens.

A nurse comes in, frowning when she looks between us all. "Is everything all right in here?"

"No," my father yells. "I want them out of here. Call security if you have to."

I don't even wait to hear the nurse's reaction. I rush out of the room, not even looking back to see if Carter is following me, because right now, I don't care.

All I care about is getting the hell out of this damn hospital.

It doesn't take long before Carter catches up, but he doesn't reach for my hand like he normally does. Instead, he stays an arm's length behind me, and when I glance back, his expression is darker than I've ever seen.

He doesn't say a word, even when we get on the empty elevator, or as we walk to the parking garage.

Anger seems to vibrate off of him, and even the people around us seem to notice, practically jumping to get out of his way as we pass.

He's furious. And he has every right to be. I can't even imagine what he thinks of me right now.

This is the moment, the one I've been dreading all along.

When this perfect little fairytale I've created with him comes crashing down around me.

Fear winds around my windpipe, making it difficult to breathe.

I knew he would react this way if he found out. I knew it would ruin everything.

When I'm in the car and he's beside me, I say shakily, "I should have told you—"

"Not now, Layla."

Those three words confirm my fear.

It's over.

CHAPTER 22

CARTER

I shut the front door a little too hard behind me. The sound resonates through the house.

Layla winces, but she doesn't say anything, and just starts up the stairs towards the bedrooms.

I let her go, because I need some time to process everything that just happened. I know I should go to her. Comfort her. But right now, I'm too fucking angry to do anything but pace, and maybe smash my hands through a wall.

It took all of my strength not to hit the man.

The man was right, he wasn't her father. Because no real father would ever treat their child the way he treated Layla. I don't care what kind of trouble she got herself into when she was younger.

Rubbing my temples, I lean against the kitchen counter and try to process what the man had said.

Layla had been pregnant before. That much is obvious. A lot of things make sense now. And yet, I know there's so much more to the story. And I need to know. I need to know what she's been holding back. Not because it will change anything, but because I think it's the key to her finally letting go of the pain she's holding on to.

I take the stairs, my footsteps heavy, and try to release the tension that's still inside of me, spinning around like molten lava, ready to explode.

Deep breath.

This isn't about you. This is about her and her asshole parents.

She won't tell me anything if I walk in there like a raging bull demanding answers.

I knock once, then open the door, freezing when I see the half-filled suitcase on her bed. "What are you doing?"

She flinches, but doesn't turn around, and just continues to pull items out of her drawer.

"Layla, stop." I grab her wrists gently. "Don't run from me."

"I…" She sucks in a shaky breath and looks away.

Taking the clothes in her hand, I place them on the bed and then pull her into my arms. Her body is tense, every muscle like steel. I rub her back until I feel her slowly relax.

"I know I should have told you." Her voice is shaky, and I can hear how hard she's trying to hold back her emotions. "I just didn't want you to see me…like they do."

I tuck my thumb under her chin and force her face up, but she keeps her eyes closed. "Look at me, Layla."

Slowly, her lashes flutter open, and she meets my gaze.

My chest tightens painfully at what I see there.

Shame.

Hurt.

Regret.

"I'm not judging you for what happened in the past."

"But…" She blinks hard, her mouth tightening in a thin line, and shakes her head. "You were so angry."

"Not at you, sweetheart." I press my lips against her fore-head and rest there for a few moments, trying to regain my composure. "He had no right to speak to you the way he did. *No one* ever has that right."

Her small hands are balled into fists on my chest. She shakes her head, and I can feel all the emotions she's trying so desperately to hold in oozing to the surface.

"Come here." I move the suitcase, placing it on the floor, then sit down on the bed and hold my hand out for her.

She just stares at it for a long moment before gradually moving towards me, her eyes downcast. When she sits, it's on the edge of the bed, far enough away from me that we're not touching.

"I'm sorry I pushed you to go today."

"You didn't know." Her fingers pick at an invisible thread on her pants.

"Do you want to tell me now?"

Her eyes close and she sighs heavily. For a long time, she doesn't say anything, and the silence is painful as I watch all sorts of tortured emotions cross her beautiful face.

Finally, her mouth opens and she says quietly, "I was fourteen when I started…seeing James."

I try my best not to react, but I see her wince when my breath comes out a little too heavy.

"I'd always been taught that it was a sin to be with anyone before marriage. And I believed it." Her voice is monotonous, her gaze staring blankly at a spot on the wall as she says the words like she's telling someone else's story, with a sort of detachment. "I didn't rebel. I was a good daughter." Her mouth curls slightly in a cynical smile. "Did my chores, got good grades, never talked back to my parents. Did all the things I was supposed to do."

There's more silence, and I can feel her shutting down.

"How did you meet him?" I ask, hoping to keep her talking.

"James?" She shakes her head and laughs darkly. "Church, if you can believe it. He was the leader of the youth group I was involved with." She closes her eyes again. "We were friends. Or I thought we were. I'd always had a huge crush on him. All the girls did. He was part of the worship team. Kind of a rock star in the community. And being older, I kind of idolized him."

"How much older?" My stomach constricts, already knowing I'm not going to like her answer.

"Twenty-four."

"Shit." I drag my fingers through my hair, fresh anger burning in my chest. "And you were fourteen."

She nods, brows pressed tightly together.

I have to ask the question eating away at me. "Did he force you?"

"No." Her expression is hard now, almost numb. "I knew what I was doing."

"At fourteen, I doubt it."

She shrugs. "I was old enough to know better, but too young to know how to really protect myself."

"And..." I grind my back teeth together. "He didn't use anything?"

"I know it sounds stupid, but I don't know. It only happened a few times. After that, he started acting weird around me. I think he knew it was wrong."

"Of course he fucking knew it was wrong. He was a grown man and you were a child."

She pulls into herself and I immediately regret losing my temper.

"You're right," she says quietly. "But no one else saw it that way. Especially not my parents. And when they found out that I was..."

God, the pain in her eyes is gutting me.

"You were pregnant?" I know it's what she wants to tell me, what I already know. But I can see how painful it is for her to say the word, so I offer it for her.

"I'd just turned fifteen. It was my mom who realized it first. I was too stupid, too naive to see the changes in my body. By the time she took me to the abortion clinic, I was too far along to terminate the pregnancy. The funny thing..." She chuckles darkly, but there's no humor in it. "Is that we'd stood outside that same clinic multiple times with our church protesting women's rights. But she had no problem killing her own grandchild in order to protect her precious image."

There's the anger that should be there. The anger she's been holding back, trapped under all her own guilt and shame.

"I thought she'd send me away. You know, to one of those places they send pregnant girls." Her eyes are vacant, and she stares ahead, reliving whatever nightmare she went though. "Without a legal option, my parents took it on themselves to...terminate the pregnancy."

Every muscle in my body tenses.

What the fuck does that mean?

A sick feeling settles over me.

"What did they do?"

Her lips tighten and she looks at me then. "Do you really want to know?"

"Yes." I have to bite the word out, because there's a part of me that doesn't. A part of me that knows I may not be able to hold back my anger if I do. "Tell me. I want to know everything."

I need to know everything. It's the only way she'll ever truly be able to move on. If we work through these things together.

"My mother tried different herbs. High doses of laxatives. Scalding baths. None of them worked. Only made me sick." She rubs her arms and shivers. "My father finally took things into his own hands."

Fuck.

She goes quiet. Too quiet.

"Layla?"

Her eyes are blank, clouded, and cold. This is where I don't want her to be. As much as I hate seeing her in pain, it's better that she let it all out.

"Tell me." It's not a request. Because of the distance she's put between us right now, I know she'll only respond to my demand.

There's a long drag of silence, then she says, "He hit me."

That's what I was afraid of. There is no way in hell I'm going to be able to hold back on the man if I ever see him again.

"Nothing happened the first time. Or the second." She's shivering now, and it's taking all my strength not to pull her into my arms. But every time I even move a fraction of an inch towards her, she flinches. "By the third day, I started to bleed. Even when I was contracting, when the...baby was being expelled from my body, he forced me to kneel at the edge of my bed and pray for forgiveness."

"My God, Layla." Coldness settles over me, and I have to blink back the tears that sting my eyes.

"God had nothing to do with it." Her words are filled with acid.

"No. You're right."

I understand now why this child is so important to her. Why she wouldn't even contemplate getting rid of it. Not that I'd ever wanted her to. But in some ways, it would have made things easier. It just would have destroyed her in the process.

"And afterwards?" I ask, trying to keep her talking. This is the most she's ever opened up to me, and I don't take it lightly.

"My parents tried to keep it a secret. But people talk. Someone must have seen us at the abortion clinic because, soon, the whole town was talking about the Harpers' slutty daughter who seduced the youth pastor. After that, I fell apart."

I don't care that she protests, I pull her against my chest and wrap my arms around her tightly. She struggles against my hold for a few seconds before finally submitting, and she goes lax in my arms.

"Those people are judgmental bastards. And your parents..." My back teeth clench so hard I swear they're going to crack. "What they did was...criminal."

"I know that now." She shivers, and I see the goosebumps that mark her arms. "Maybe I always did. When I was strong enough, I ran."

"At fifteen?" I rub her arms, trying to imagine myself at fifteen. There's no way in hell I would have lasted a week on my own, let alone seven years.

"I haven't seen either of my parents again until today."

I feel like such an asshole right now. Pushing her to go, after everything that they did to her.

"You should have told me. I would never have made you go." Threading my fingers with hers, I bring her hand to my lips and kiss each knuckle.

"No. You were right. I needed to see her one last time. I know in her own twisted way she was trying to protect me."

I don't say what I really think. Instead, I just hold her and press my lips into her hair.

The sound of the old clock in the hallway, and Layla's shallow, uneven breaths, are the only noises I hear for a long time.

"I didn't sleep with anyone else until Travis," she says, shocking the hell out of me. "I know you probably won't believe me–"

"I do." I cup her chin and twist to look at her. "I knew who you were the first day I saw you. Good. Pure. Innocent."

She shakes her head and squeezes her eyes tightly shut. "I'm none of those things. I haven't been for a very long time."

Fat tears slide down her face.

"Yes." I drag my thumbs across her cheeks, wiping away her tears. "You are. None of what you've told me changes that."

"When I found out I was pregnant again, I was so scared. But then, I thought…maybe it was a second chance. I know it's silly. I'm still an unwed mother having an unplanned pregnancy, and I know it's going to change everything in my life, but this time I get a choice."

"It's not silly. And you're *not* alone." I kiss her forehead, her eyelids, her nose, her mouth, needing her to know that I'm not going anywhere. That I'm hers, just as much as she's mine.

When I press my mouth against hers, her lips are hard against mine. But slowly, she begins to return my kiss. Soon, her body relaxes, and I can feel the tension melting away.

"Marry me," I murmur, stroking her hair.

"What?" She pulls back and frowns.

"Marry me. Be my wife."

She shakes her head. "After everything I've told you? Why?"

"Because I love you. More than I've ever loved anyone or anything in my life. I know it's messy, and there'll be bumps ahead, but I want to make this thing real between us. Legal and binding."

Her brows are drawn down, and she's frowning at me. Not the reaction I was hoping for.

"You're serious?"

"More serious than I've been about anything in my life." I place my hand on her stomach. "And I want this child to be mine."

She tilts her head, her gaze narrowing. "Carter—"

"Listen to me before you say anything. Travis has already signed the papers. There's nothing stopping me from claiming the child as mine." Entwining our fingers, I rest my forehead against hers. "We'll be a family."

Her lips part, and her eyes close. She whispers, "You're too good to me."

There's an ache in my chest that warns me she's going to say no. That she's still going to run from me.

"I just…"

Shit. Here it comes. Whatever excuse she's made now to reaffirm her delusional idea that she's not worthy of more.

She exhales an uneven breath. "I think it's best—"

"Okay." Frustration seeps into my voice, constricting my throat.

I'm a confident guy. Maybe even verging on arrogant. But I can't help the insecurities that creep unwarranted into the back of my mind.

Maybe she doesn't feel the same way about me. Maybe there's a part of her that hopes Travis comes back. Maybe she's just with me because she's afraid to be alone.

I drag my fingers through my hair and lean back against the headboard, rubbing my eyes.

"I'm sorry," she mutters.

The best I can do right now is give her a weak smile. Swinging my legs over the side of the bed, I start to stand. "I'll go make us something to eat."

"Wait." Her fingers wrap around my wrist, and she blinks

up at me, her soft brown eyes full of all the emotion she's holding back. "Don't go."

She's still sitting on the edge of the bed, and I move so that I'm standing between her legs. Her fingers immediately hook around the belt loops of my jeans.

Brushing my knuckles across her cheek, I sigh. "You haven't eaten since lunch."

"I'm not hungry." She chews on her bottom lip, then says, "I just…need you."

That's as much of an admission as she's ever given me. "You have me."

Her fingers move to my belt, unhooking it.

"Layla," I growl, my hands moving to her hair when I see the intent in her eyes. I know her emotions are all over the place, but I understand her need. I feel it, too. The need to reconnect, emotionally and physically. The need to know that everything is all right between us.

She is the air that I breathe. Without her, I am certain I would cease to exist. If being with her means only getting half of her heart, then it's the way it's going to have to be. Because there's no way in hell I can walk away.

And maybe the marriage thing is just my way of making sure she can't either.

I groan as her hands work my jeans and boxer briefs over my hips, and my cock springs free, already hard and heavy with wanting her.

My heart hammers in my chest when she looks up at me. God, those eyes. So fucking expressive. They tell me everything I need to know. She may not be able to say it yet, but she cares about me, maybe even loves me. And I sure as hell know she wants me.

Her fingers wrap around the long length of my erection and she licks her lips, before her warm mouth takes me in. She braces herself with one hand, holding onto my hip as her tongue flicks the sensitive underside of my cock.

"You have no idea what you do to me," I groan, cupping her face as she takes me deeper into her sweet little mouth. My balls draw up tight to my body.

Watching her is pure, erotic bliss.

"Come here," I growl out, pulling her hair back gently, so my cock slides from her mouth with a little pop.

She stands up, and I help her when she starts to pull at my shirt, reaching back and pulling it over my head.

Her fingers instantly go to the ink on my chest, like they always do, then she looks up, eyes brimming with emotion. "I love you, Carter."

I swear, my heart stops in my chest, and time stands still.

No three words have ever sounded better, but I can see the 'but' forming on her lips.

I capture the word with my mouth before it has a chance to escape. I won't let her ruin this moment with her fears.

This moment is mine.

She loves me. Part of me already knew it. But to hear her say it does something inside of me. Both placating and spurring on the beast that wants to possess and consume her.

I run my fingers down the curve of her neck. She shivers and makes the sweetest noise. A mix between a moan and a sigh. The sound has my balls tightening so hard, my cock throbs with need.

I need her naked. Need her bared to me. Need to not just hear the words, but feel them in her touch.

CHAPTER 23

LAYLA

*O*nce the words are out of my mouth, I know there's no taking them back. I've never told anyone except my parents that I love them. Because until now, I know I never have. Not really. Not like this.

Carter's mouth is on me, stopping my argument, my reasoning as to why this thing between us will never work. And right now, I don't care. All I care about is his touch. The feel of his skin against mine. The need to be filled with something other than the pain that's been squeezing at my chest since we left the hospital.

I know I'm using him, using sex to drive away those demons from my mind, but it's all I can do to stop from falling apart completely.

Rough fingers rake across my skin as he quickly undresses me, his own desire evident in the tightness of his features and the urgency of his kiss.

"Say it again," he growls when we're both standing naked, his thick, throbbing erection pressing against my stomach.

"I love you." It's easier this time, and doesn't come out sounding as forced.

His mouth crashes down on mine, demanding and possessive.

I press against his strong, muscular chest and I lose myself in his mouth. His tongue snakes between my lips and it takes all that I have not to lose myself completely in him.

It would be easy to give up control. Let him have me in every way. Heart. Body. Mind. Soul.

Marry me. Those words tremble through me.

The moment I found out I was pregnant, I gave up all hope that I'd ever find someone who would want me, let alone marry me.

God, I want it. I want all the promises and dreams he's offering. But there's still a part of me that knows no matter how good his intentions are, he wouldn't be asking me to make that commitment if I weren't having a baby.

Maybe it shouldn't matter. But it does.

"Stop thinking," he murmurs in my ear, grabbing my hips as he turns and sits on the edge of the bed. He pulls me down so that I'm straddling him, my knees against his hips.

His erection strains against me, and I can practically feel it pulsating against my stomach.

I wrap my arm around his shoulders, and press my forehead against his, taking a few deep breaths.

"I've got you, sweetheart," he says softly, kissing my neck, jaw, and lips. His scruff is scratchy and wonderfully rough against my skin. "Just let go."

One large palm runs up my back, the other supports my weight, gripping my hip as I begin to grind against him, the friction causing him to groan.

He's holding back now, waiting for me.

I'm already wet for him, and when I lift myself on my knees and nudge against the thick head of his cock, the last bit of restraint that's holding me back releases.

With a gasp of pleasure, I dig my fingers into his hair and slide down on him, allowing him to fill me completely.

Burning pleasure ripples through me, and a low guttural groan vibrates from Carter's chest. His fingers tighten, digging into my flesh, holding me still as he kisses me, giving me time to adjust to his size.

"You have no idea what you do to me." His breathing is harsh, his words thick with desire. "If you did, you would never have any doubts."

I kiss him back, hard, my chest clenching at his words, searing my emotions. His teeth nip at me, catching my lower lip. He strokes his tongue over it with a teasing lick.

His mouth remains on mine, one hand supporting me as he moves us back on the bed. He's still inside of me, throbbing against my walls, and my clit pulses and aches, demanding friction.

Palms pressed on his strong shoulders, I start to move. Slowly at first, small, grinding strokes that only add fuel to the growing fire building between us.

He tilts his head up, catching my breast in his mouth, nipping and licking, and sending pulses of electricity to my core.

Each touch is spiked with lust and love, a mixture that creates an inferno of heat that builds within me, blazing across my skin.

Desperation fills me and I move faster, demanding more. He's both tender and demanding, pushing me over the edge.

"Carter," I cry out, my head tilting back, eyes clenching shut, allowing his touch to drive my demons back to the darkest pit of myself where they belong.

He moves with me, his hips thrusting upward as his

hands guide my movements to the perfect rhythm we've created.

This is happiness, and I let myself feel it. Really feel it. Without all the anxiety and fear that usually holds me back.

My body explodes around him, wave after wave of intense pleasure bursting through me, blinding me. A strangled sound erupts from the deepest part of me, and I'm falling, my body weightless, yet filled with such complete ecstasy that I don't care if I ever come down from the incredible high.

Inside me, I feel his hard release, and hear his guttural moan as his orgasm sends one last intense ripple of pleasure through my core.

Spent and exhausted, I collapse on top of him, careful not to put too much pressure on my stomach.

We lay there like that for a short time, before I slowly roll to my side, allowing him to wrap an arm around me.

"I love you," he whispers, brushing my hair away from my cheek. "Do you believe me when I tell you that?"

I nod, because I do. I just don't know if it's enough.

"Thank you for the library," I say, remembering the gift he'd given me this morning.

His lips lift in a small grin. "You're welcome."

Running my fingers over his chest, another surge of warmth spreads through me. I know what it is – hope.

"About what you asked me earlier…"

His muscles tense slightly under my touch. "Yeah?"

I can't give him the answer he wants. Not right now, but I want to give him something. "Maybe…"

He presses a kiss into my hair and exhales a heavy breath.

"Maybe is better than no," he says lightly.

I nod, wishing I could give him more. Because with him, life is good. Really good. The fairytale, happily ever after good. And it's terrifying the crap out of me. Because one thing I've learned in my life, the one true constant, is that disaster is always hiding just around the corner.

CHAPTER 24

CARTER

"*W*hat the fuck?" A deep, guttural cry pushes into my dreams.

My entire body jolts awake, adrenaline spiking through my veins, preparing me to fight whatever danger is waiting for me.

I sit up, blinking hard until my eyes adjust to the morning light. When I do, I curse under my breath, because Travis is standing at the edge of the bed, a deep scowl twisting his features as he glares down at Layla, who stirs beside me.

The bed creaks as I start to shift. "Keep your voice down."

"Keep my voice down?" he repeats, blinking at me like I'm insane, his face blistering with rage.

"Go," I say quietly, but the warning is still there. "We'll talk downstairs."

"Are you kidding me? I want to know what the hell is going on. Right now," he yells, his blue eyes wide with bewilderment and anger.

Layla comes fully awake, and she gasps when her gaze falls on Travis. I can see all the fear that I've been working so hard to get rid of these past months fill her. She clutches the blankets to her chest, and her eyes are wide as she stares back at my brother.

"Jesus, Layla." Travis drags his fingers through his long hair, his face red with anger.

She sucks in an uneven breath. "Travis, I didn't mean–"

"You really are a dirty little slut. You couldn't have my cock, so you jump right into bed with my brother."

"Watch yourself," I growl, grabbing my pants from the floor. I shove my legs into them as quickly as I can, needing to get him the hell away from her.

Already, I can see her shutting down. Her shoulders sag, and resignation fills her expression.

Travis' hands ball into fists at his side, but his anger is only directed at Layla. "How long did it take before you were screwing him? One week? Two?"

"Shut the fuck up before you say something that makes me want to hit you more than I already do."

Travis looks at me then, his anger fixed on me, where it should be. "You're seriously fucking her?"

"Downstairs," I growl out, pointing to the opened door. "Now."

"Un-fucking-believable." He shakes his head, still scowling, but thankfully he listens to me, turning and walking out of the bedroom while mumbling a series of curses.

I wince at the sound of his heavy footsteps as they clomp down the stairs.

Layla's face is pale, her eyes vacant. There are no tears, just a hollowness that scares the shit out of me.

"It's going to be okay," I say, leaning over the bed and placing my hand under her chin, forcing her to look at me.

No reaction.

I press my lips against hers, but she doesn't return my kiss.

"Let me deal with him. Just stay here."

Again, nothing. Just a blank stare that makes my blood go cold.

I've never wanted to hurt someone more in my life than I want to hurt Travis right now.

I shut my bedroom door behind me when I leave, hoping it'll muffle the words that I'm about to have with my brother.

Layla doesn't need or deserve this shit right now. Especially not when she's so close to her due date. Any stress could cause her to go into labor at any moment.

Travis is in the living room, and when he sees me, he stops his pacing and points his finger at me. "Do you have any idea how fucked up this is?"

"Just shut your mouth and listen. It's not what you think."

"So you're not screwing her? You were what? Having a little slumber party butt ass naked?" The sarcasm drips from his words.

"I'm in love with her."

That shuts him up. At least, for a few seconds, then he growls, "Bullshit. I come back here, wanting to make things better. To do what you said, and take responsibility. And you're what? Playing house with the mother of my child."

"*You* walked away."

"I came back," he shouts, fire blazing in his eyes. "And you knew I would. I just needed time to think. To get my head straight."

His words are like a punch to the gut. He's right, there was always a part of me that knew he'd come back eventually. Because, as selfish and egotistical as he is, he's not a complete asshole. I knew that his sense of obligation would eventually kick in.

But that doesn't mean he loves Layla, or even that he wants the kid.

I do. More than anything else in the world.

"You don't want this." I try to keep my tone even, my temper in check. "You told me yourself that you aren't mature enough to have a kid–"

"So, you thought it was your obligation to step in and take my place?"

"It wasn't like that–"

"Right. You love her." He laughs darkly. "Give me a break."

"I *do* love her. And I'm going to make her my wife."

That gets his attention. His eyes widen and his face drains of color.

"You're kidding me, right?" There's panic in his expression now. "You can't do that. Do you know how messed up that would be?"

"We'll make it work."

"Bullshit." He starts to pace again, fingers clenching and unclenching like he wants to hit something. "This. You. Her. All of it is fucking bullshit."

"You're the one who left. Not Layla. Not me. You gave up your rights to come stomping in here on your high horse and point fingers."

"It's *my* fucking kid."

"You're right." Layla stands on the first stair, her light brown hair pulled back in a ponytail, and her fitted t-shirt stretched taut across her rounded stomach. The distress in her voice strikes me hard, and I can feel the pain in her words when she admits, "It is."

I open my mouth to argue, then clamp it shut.

Mine. Every possessive bone in my body screams it.

I narrow my eyes at her, praying she isn't saying what I think she is.

Travis starts towards her, and I have to hold myself back

from tackling him to the ground. I know he won't lay a hand on her, but it doesn't stop me from not wanting him anywhere near her.

"Why did you come back?" Layla asks, all her focus on Travis, her expression still stoic.

"To fix things." He stands a few feet away from her now, his back to me. "I shouldn't have left. I know that now. I thought...I thought we could try." He shakes his head fervently. "But this is just insane."

Layla doesn't respond. She just watches him, the only indication of distress being the small muscle in her jaw twitching.

"So what happens? You two get hitched, and then I'm what? Uncle Travis?" He turns and looks at me with pure hatred in his eyes. "Or are we both going to play Daddy?" He laughs and throws his hands up. "That'll be fun explaining to people."

"You think I give two shits what people think?" I say, the truth not as clear cut. Because the fact is, I don't want Travis in this child's life. I know how fucking selfish that is. But over the past several months, I've come to think of it as mine.

Having him around would do more than complicate things, it would change things between Layla and me. Because I can see it in her eyes that she's already pulling away, already thinking about her escape route.

Layla sits down on the step, and even though I can tell she's trying her best to hold herself together, her hand shakes when she reaches for the railing.

"I need a drink," Travis says, despite it only being a little past eight in the morning. He turns on his heels and storms into the kitchen.

Layla flinches when cupboard doors start to slam.

"Where the hell is all the alcohol?" Travis' breathing is harsh, his tone desperate.

"There isn't any," I say, not tearing my gaze away from Layla, whose arms are wrapped protectively around herself.

"Of course, there isn't. Saint fucking Carter, my ass," Travis hisses.

"Where are you going?" I bark as he starts towards the front door.

"What do you care? It's pretty obvious you're just itching to get rid of me again. I hope it's worth it. Choosing a little tramp over your own brother. Mom and Dad would be so proud–"

My fist slams into his face, silencing him. His head snaps back and he stumbles, blood instantly oozing from his nose.

"Carter, stop!" Layla shrieks behind me.

I'm prepared for Travis' retaliation, but not for the look of betrayal and hurt that meets me when he finally gets his bearings.

He wipes the blood from his nose with the back of his hand, his lips tight, and jaw clenched. "You're an asshole, you know that?"

My chest squeezes painfully.

Travis turns and storms out of the house, slamming the door so hard behind him that the pictures on the wall rattle.

I rub my knuckles, staring at the closed door for a few seconds before turning back to Layla.

"You shouldn't have hit him." There's emotion in her voice now, tears glistening in her eyes.

"He deserved it. No one talks to you like that."

"He had a reason to. Think about it from his perspective. He comes home to find us...together."

"He walked away," I say incredulously.

"And he came back."

Cold trickles down my back. *What is she saying?*

"You're not thinking about giving him a second chance?"

"It's his child. I can't–"

149

"He signed the papers, made his decision." Fear constricts in my chest, tightening my throat.

"He's your brother." Her hands reach for the railing, fingers trembling. "You're the one who told me he'd be back. Are you really prepared to cut him out of your life...for me?"

She has no clue what I'm willing to do for her.

"Yes," I growl, moving towards her, but she puts out a hand to stop me when I try to touch her.

"You say that now, but..." A small, sad smile draws her lips up, her expression unreadable.

Every insecurity that I've tried to suppress fills me.

She wants him.

Wants to raise this child with him.

I was just a second choice.

Somewhere deep inside of me, I know it's not true, but then there's the other voice, the one that's screaming at me right now, telling me what a blind idiot I've been.

I came swooping in here, not giving her much, if any, choice. Demanding that she be mine.

She told me that Travis was only the second person she's been with. He had to mean something to her. I'd tried not to think about that. But the evidence of what was between them would always be there. If Travis really had changed his mind, then I couldn't stop him from being a part of the child's life. Being a part of Layla's.

Fuck.

My head is spinning.

I need to get out of here before I say something I'll regret. I take her hand and stroke my thumb across the soft skin.

God, I love her. I thought I knew how much, but I really didn't, not until now, when I'm about to lose her.

The question is, do I love her enough to give her what she needs? Even if what she needs is for me to walk away?

"I'll go."

"What?" Her gaze jerks up to mine.

"Travis left his bags." I nod at the duffle bag and knapsack by the front door. "He'll be back. And you two need to talk."

"Carter—"

"There are some things I've been putting off in New York. I'll go there for a few days. Give you time to think about what you want."

I take her hand and brush my lips against her knuckles. Every cell in my body prays that she'll try and stop me.

But she doesn't.

CHAPTER 25

LAYLA

I should have stopped Carter from leaving. I know that. My heart shattered into a million pieces when I watched him walk out the door.

I've spent the rest of the day regretting it. Every few minutes, I look at my cell phone, hoping that he'll call. Or I glance at the front door, praying that he'll walk through it.

Call him, my heart screams. But my brain doesn't let me, because I know that Carter is right, I do need to talk to Travis, and it's probably best that he isn't here when I do.

I rub my hands over my bare arms when I look at Travis' bags, still sitting at the front entrance. It's late, past ten, and he still hasn't come back. Maybe he won't for a few days. He has other places to stay, and I'm sure he has a lot to process.

Loneliness surrounds me like a cold blanket, and I shiver.

The house is so quiet, but it's not just that. When Carter is here, even if he's just working on his laptop, the place is always filled with his presence. Like a warmth that I can feel in every room. But I don't feel that now. I just feel empty.

I should go to bed, and I did try, but the second I lay down, Carter's lingering scent made my emotions go all erratic, and I had to get up or I'd end up crying myself to sleep.

It's going to be all right, my heart cries, but my head counters, *This is what I warned you about.*

With a heavy sigh, I walk into the kitchen and grab the orange juice out of the fridge, wincing when I feel a small pain in my side. I rub the spot, feeling the baby move beneath my palm.

Three more weeks and he or she will be here. That's what I should be focusing on, not the fact that I may be losing the only person in my life who has ever cared about me. The only man that I've ever loved.

I pick up my phone that's sitting on the counter and check my messages.

Nothing.

Swallowing hard, I scroll to his number. I need to hear his voice. I need to tell him I love him, that no matter what happens with Travis, that won't change. I'm about to press dial, when I hear the front door open. It slams shut.

"Carter?" I put my phone back on the counter, hope surging through me. But by the heaviness of the steps and the uneven gate, I know it's not him even before Travis storms into the kitchen.

A prick of fear needles across my flesh.

"Where is he?" Breathing hard, he takes a few threatening steps towards me. There's something in his eyes, a brightness that doesn't look right. When I don't answer right away, he yells, "Where is he?"

I flinch, which only seems to make him angrier.

"Carter went to New York for a few days. Why don't you sit down, and I'll make a pot of coffee. We can talk."

"You want to talk?" His lips pull up in a sneer, and he corners me against the counter. "Okay. Let's talk. How about we start with whether that's really my kid."

My breath hitches, not just because of the accusation, but because of the way he's trapping me. It sends off warning signals in my brain. I'd never think Travis would hurt me—or anyone else, for that matter—but right now, he isn't in his right mind. That's obvious.

He doesn't smell like alcohol, but I can tell he's not sober. And he's clearly looking for a fight.

"You know it is."

"I don't know shit." He grabs my wrist, twisting just enough to cause pain but not enough to do any real damage. "Not about you. But I did a little digging when I was away. Had a buddy look into your past. And it looks like you weren't as sweet and innocent as you led everyone to believe. You had quite the reputation in Springcreek."

"Travis, you're hurting me." I try to stay calm despite my growing panic.

"I'll admit it. You're good." He gets in my face, his breath hot and stale on my cheek. He doesn't release me. Instead, his grip tightens, and I know it'll leave a bruise. "You couldn't have me, so you played my brother."

"It's not like that."

"Right. You two are in *love*," he snorts, and he moves closer to me so that his body is pressed hard against my stomach. "Were you in love with me, too? How about the poor bastard that got you knocked up the first time?"

"Travis, please." I try to push him away, but he doesn't budge.

He's not as big as Carter, but he's strong, and I'm not

really in any condition to fight him off. My first and only priority is to keep my baby safe.

"Or maybe that was your plan all along? Using me to get to him?" His fingers dig into my flesh. "Thought you could bag yourself a rich husband by sleeping with his brother."

His accusations don't even make any sense. It's like he's trying to find any and every excuse to think the worst of me.

"I didn't mean for any of this to happen."

"Bullshit." He releases me, and I see his fist flying towards my face.

Oh God. All I can do is brace for the impact. I pinch my eyes closed and pull back.

Crunch.

The sound of wood splintering in my ear makes me cry out.

Travis pulls his bloody hand out of the broken cupboard door, without so much as a wince.

I know he's on something now.

"You took my brother away from me."

"No. Carter loves you. He'd do anything for you."

"Like raise my kid. Or marry the slut who I got knocked up." Blood trickles from his hand to the floor, and already it's swollen to twice its original size.

"This isn't you talking. You're not like this."

"You took everything from me. My home. My freedom. My fucking brother." He laughs, a hysterical sound, then picks up a glass from the counter and throws it across the room. It shatters on impact. "You fucked my fucking brother."

I need to get away from him.

Not caring about the tiny shards of glass that cut into my feet, I run out of the room towards the stairs.

Panic.

Fear.

They narrow my vision, and make my legs feel like jelly.

I'm not sure if Travis follows me, I just run. Hard and fast. Until a sharp pain slices across my stomach, buckling me over, and a gush of something warm and sticky rushes down my leg.

I can't breathe. Can't scream.

Pain.

Pain.

Pain.

That's all there is, blinding and paralyzing.

When I finally catch my breath, I reach between my legs and pull my fingers back.

Blood.

Thick and red, it runs heavily down my legs, staining the pink pajama bottoms I'm wearing. It begins pooling at my feet.

No. No. No.

This can't be happening.

A strangled sound comes from my throat.

"Oh my God, Layla." Travis' hands are on me now, and I try to push him away. "Shit. I didn't mean to hurt you."

"Call Carter. Please."

"Okay. Just sit down." He takes my elbow and helps me down to the floor, hovering over me like he doesn't know what to do.

Another stab of pain, like my stomach is being shredded from the inside, causes me to gasp, and my vision darkens.

"Call him," I cry.

"Okay."

I lay down on the floor, pressing my cheek against the cool wood. Nausea rolls over me, mixing with the sense of impending doom. It's a strange feeling. Fear and panic begin to fade, replaced by a sense of detachment. Like I'm floating somewhere on the edge of consciousness.

Stay awake, Layla. I bite my lip hard, tasting blood. Anything to keep from fading into the emptiness that threatens to consume me.

"He's not answering." Panic edges Travis' voice.

I can feel myself losing consciousness. I blink, and my vision goes blurry. One black spot appears, followed by another.

I can't lose this baby.

"What do I do?" Travis is kneeling beside me, his blue eyes now sober. But they're so full of alarm that he seems frozen, unable to doing anything.

"Call…911," I choke out, struggling to stay conscious.

I'm going to die. I can feel it – death. A cold darkness presses in, ready to take me. Blackness swims through my sight, sucking me under, until it's all I know.

CHAPTER 26

CARTER

I couldn't go to New York. Something in the back of my mind warned me not to. And the minute I pull up to the house, I know I was right to listen to that voice inside my head.

The front door is slightly ajar, but the house is dark.

I flip on the hallway light and my heart stops.

Fresh blood stains the hardwood. And it seems to be everywhere.

No.

"Layla," I scream her name as I race from room to room, flipping on the lights.

The living room is empty, and so is the dining room. Taking two steps at a time, I slam open the bedroom doors, and then the bathroom door, but there's no sign of her.

"Layla," I keep shouting, praying that there's some mistake. That she'll answer me.

My body goes ice cold when I walk into the kitchen and

my shoes crunch on the broken glass beneath them. One of the cupboard doors is smashed in, and a chair lies on its side in the middle of the room.

Travis. I have no doubt that he did this. Rage and fear boil inside of me.

God, I should never have left her.

I pull out my cell. The battery is dead.

"Fuck."

There's a landline in the living room, but my fingers shake when I press the numbers to dial my brother.

He picks up on the first ring. "Carter? Thank God–"

"What the fuck did you do to her?" I scream. "Where is she?"

"I've been trying to call you." I can hear the guilt in his voice, which only confirms my worst fears.

This time when I speak, my voice is low and dangerous. "Where the fuck is she, Travis?"

I hear him swallow hard before saying, "University Hospital. They took her straight into–"

I don't let him finish. I just hang up, and race to the car. I speed through the city, going through at least two red lights, and parking in a no-parking zone in front of the emergency doors.

Let them tow me.

"Layla Harper," I say to the receptionist at the front desk, trying not to betray my panic, but it's nearly impossible. "I need to know where she is."

"One moment." It takes what seems like an eternity for her to check her computer. She frowns at the screen, making my chest squeeze, then looks up at me. "Are you family?"

"I'm her husband." It's a small lie now, but the moment she gets out of this damn place, I'm going to make it a reality.

Her lips tighten before saying, "She's in surgery right now."

I groan, a gut-wrenching sound that has the woman looking at me with sympathy.

"There's a private waiting room set aside for her family. Here..." She scribbles a number on a pad and hands it to me. "Just take the elevators to the fourth floor and make a left."

I start towards the elevators, pushing the button impatiently until the doors open. I'm aware of the looks I'm getting, and I know if I don't calm down, someone is going to call security.

She's going to be all right. She has to be. I'm not helping her by freaking out when I don't know what happened. But the second I see my brother, I lose my fucking mind.

Travis is sitting alone in the small waiting room, his head in one hand, cradling the other injured one in his lap. He looks up at me when I walk in. His expression drips with guilt, his face stricken and pale.

Blood stains his pants and his shirt.

Layla's blood.

Remorse is all over his face, but I don't care.

He starts to stand. "Carter, I'm sorry–"

I grab him by the collar of his shirt, picking him up and slamming him against the wall. "What did you do?"

He doesn't fight back, just goes limp in my arms. "I didn't mean to hurt her."

"But you did," I hiss.

"No." He shakes his head adamantly. "I didn't hit her. I promise. Yeah, I lost my temper. Said things I shouldn't have. But I swear to God, I didn't hurt her. She ran out of the room, then the next thing I knew she was bent over, and there was...blood."

His eyes are glassy, his face distorted in a grimace, and even though I don't want to believe him, I do.

"I was fucked up." He drags his good hand through his hair. "I still am."

"What are you on?"

"I went to a buddy's house. I only did one line, but–"

"Cocaine?" I drop my hands and look at him in disgust.

"I know. Shit." He sits down on the couch. "I'm sorry."

There's a knock, and both our heads jerk in the direction of the door. A small middle-aged woman wearing scrubs frowns when she glances between us.

"Which one of you is the father?" she asks.

Me, I want to say. Instead, I grind my teeth and look at Travis.

Something passes between us, and I see the final acceptance in his eyes.

"He is," Travis says, nodding at me.

The doctor doesn't look convinced, but she sighs and addresses me. "We had to do an emergency C-section. Her placenta detached from the uterus, and she sustained significant blood loss."

I can't breathe. Can't move. I'm just waiting for the woman to tell me that Layla is gone. That she didn't make it.

"She'll be in post-op for a few hours."

"She's okay?" The words come out in a rush.

"We're still monitoring her, but she's stable now."

"Thank God." My hands are ice cold and shaking as I wring them together. She's okay. She's going to be fine. I glance up at the doctor. "And the baby?"

She smiles then. "He's healthy. You can see him now, if you'd like."

He. It's a boy. Layla hadn't wanted to know what the sex was, so we hadn't found out. Neither of us cared, as long as the baby was healthy.

Behind the doctor, another woman peers into the room, looking between Travis and I nervously. "There's a police officer here asking to speak to a Travis Bennett. They have some questions about what happened."

Travis looks up at me, his face pale, and I can see the flash of hope that I'm going to somehow bail him out. When I look away, I hear the creak of the couch as he stands.

"I'm glad they're both going to be okay," he mutters, before following the woman out of the room.

The doctor is still watching me, lips pursed. "If you'll come with me, I'll take you to your son."

My son. Those two words chase away the anger that's consumed me since I walked into this room and saw Travis.

The doctor leads me through a series of corridors to a small room, where a nurse is wrapping a screaming infant in a blue and white striped blanket. She smiles at me when I approach.

"He's got quite the set of lungs," she says, motioning for me to come closer.

He's pink. That's the first thing I notice. And bald. I swear, the kid has zero hair. And what he does have is light brown like Layla's. He keeps wailing, a sound that sounds more like a sheep than a baby.

"Is he okay?"

"He's perfect." She tucks the last of his blanket around him, then picks him up and starts to hand him to me.

I hesitate. He's so damn small. I swear, I'm going to break him or drop him.

"You'll be fine. Just make sure his neck is supported." She places him in my arms, adjusting him so that his head is in the crook of my elbow.

Almost immediately, he stops crying. My breath gets locked somewhere in the back of my throat, and a rush of emotion floods through me.

"He knows who his Daddy is," she says, before moving to fill out a chart that's attached to the glass bassinette.

Emotion floods through me.

His Daddy. Tears prick at my eyes as I trace my thumb

across his small cheek, making his lips purse in a sucking motion. Damn, I can't control the way my vision blurs. Layla should be here with me, meeting our son together for the first time. Travis took that away from us. For that, I'm going to have a hard time forgiving him.

The nurse asks me a few questions as she fills out her forms. When she's done, she smiles and says, "You can stay here. This will be your wife's room once she's released from post-op."

"Do you know how long that will be?" I need to see her, and she needs to see her son. *Our son.*

"It shouldn't be that much longer."

When she starts towards the door, I realize she's about to leave me alone...*with the baby.*

"Wait." I can't hide the panic in my voice.

She turns, brows raised. "Yes?"

"What about..." I glance down at the small bundle in my arms.

I swear the woman is holding back a laugh when she says, "I'll come back and check on you. If you need anything, you can press the button on the bed."

With those brief instructions, she leaves, and I sit down in the rocking chair that's in the corner of the room, shifting the baby in my arms, which makes him baa again. One tiny fist pulls free of the blanket and shakes up at me.

"You're all right, little one." I rock him, and croon, "You're safe. And you're mine. And whether your stubborn mommy wants to admit it or not, she's mine, too."

The sound of my voice seems to soothe him, and he stops crying. His eyes open for the first time since he's been in my arms, and he looks up at me.

I keep talking, and he seems almost mesmerized by my voice. "I'm your daddy. You don't know what that means yet, but it means I'm never going to let anyone hurt you."

He yawns and his eyes close again. I'm fascinated by all his tiny movements, and his small, swollen features. He's all scrunched and wrinkled, but I'm already in love with him.

I'm not sure how much time passes before anyone comes back into the room. An hour, maybe two, but I don't put him down because he seems content in my arms. And, in all honesty, I don't want to let him go.

"Mr. Bennett?" The doctor who had spoken to me earlier comes into the room, followed by a nurse who doesn't make eye contact with me. She just reaches for the baby.

Both of the women's expressions are severe. I almost don't allow the nurse to take my son, wanting to use him as a shield to stop whatever news they've come here to give me. I know it's bad. I can see it in their eyes.

"I'm just going to feed and change him," the nurse says, giving me a look that's filled with compassion.

With a shuddering breath, I hand him to her and slowly stand, meeting the doctor's gaze.

"Layla?" I ask, my voice shaking.

"There've been some complications and we've had to take her back into surgery."

I wish I hadn't stood, because I'm pretty sure my legs are going to give out on me.

"How…what happened?"

"She's still hemorrhaging. They're trying to stop the bleeding."

I can hear the unsaid words, the seriousness of the situation.

"I thought they stopped it. You said she was going to be all right."

"She was stable, but like I said, there were complications in post-op."

Scrubbing my hands over my face, I feel like the floor is giving out on me.

"Mr. Bennett, if there are any other family members that need to be called, I suggest you call them now."

Because they're not sure if she's going to make it.

I sit down heavily.

Agony slices my chest, and I crumple forward with my face in my hands, because I realize that I may still lose her.

CHAPTER 27

CARTER

*T*wo hours turns into four, then six. No one seems to want to give me any answers.

I called Kira, and she came immediately, but she's just as freaked out as I am, and her constant tears are only stressing me out.

And I have no idea where Travis went. For all I know, the cops took him to the station to question him about what happened. Maybe they arrested him, or maybe he just took off again.

The nurses changed shifts a couple of hours ago, and I don't know the new one that comes into the room to check on the baby. The baby – he still doesn't have a name.

My throat tightens at the thought of Layla never getting to see him, never having the chance to hold him.

I meant what I promised. He's mine. No matter what happens to her, I'll raise him as my own, and love him the same. Nothing will change that. But even the possibility of doing it alone makes my heart pound painfully in my chest.

Kira paces the room, dark circles under her swollen eyes. "Why isn't anyone coming to tell us what's going on?"

I shift the baby in my arms when he starts to stir. He's going to be hungry again soon.

There's a knock on the door, and both Kira and I jump.

Max, Kira's boyfriend, pops his head in, then opens the door, carrying a tray of coffees and a brown paper bag. "I thought you could use some caffeine and food."

I know he's trying to be helpful, but I can't help but resent the casual tone in his voice.

Layla is somewhere in the damn hospital fighting for her life, and he's bringing doughnuts and bagels.

"You should eat something," Kira says. "I can hold him–"

"I'm fine," I snap, seeing the look she exchanges with Max, but I don't fucking care. All I care about is knowing what the hell is going on with the woman I love.

"She's going to be fine," Kira says, moving towards me to place a hand on my arm. "Layla's a fighter, and she has everything to live for."

All I can do is nod, because words fail me.

I pray that she's right, but when the door opens again and the doctor walks in, her expression is morose. I clench my back teeth, preparing myself for the worst.

"She's out of surgery. All we can do now is wait."

Wait. That's all I've been fucking doing.

"I need to see her."

"Just one of you," the doctor says.

"Go." Kira motions for me to hand her the baby.

Numbly, I follow the doctor.

Shock and grief hit me like a baseball bat to the chest when I see Layla. There are tubes and machines everywhere, and her face is pale – too pale. She looks so damn fragile.

"You have to fight, sweetheart," I whisper, brushing her hair away from her face. "You have to fight for me, and for our son."

Taking her hand, careful of the IV attached, I bring it to my lips and kiss each knuckle.

"Fight for our happy ending. Just don't..." Tears choke me. "Don't give up."

There's no response, and I don't expect one. The doctor told me that she's still heavily sedated, and she will be for a long time.

What I'm not prepared for is the sudden high-pitched beeping of the monitors. Almost immediately, the room is filled with people, and I'm being ushered out.

"What's going on?"

"You need to wait outside, sir."

"She's crashing," someone says, making the ground beneath me feel like it's giving away.

One glance at the heart monitor, and I see the flat line running across the screen, which only jumps when someone begins chest compressions.

"Layla," I cry out, needing to get to her, to force her to fight, to live.

"Sir, you can't be in here."

"I'm not leaving." My heart speeds up, an erratic pounding in my chest.

"You need to let us do our jobs." Her hands are on me, pushing me from the room, and the doors are being shut in my face.

God, no. This can't be the end. This isn't the way our story is supposed to unfold. I'm supposed to marry her, and we'll eventually have more children. Not this.

I lean against the cold wall and slowly slide to the floor.

Powerless.

Broken.

We never know when our lives are about to shift. Maybe if we did, we'd do things differently.

Regret curdles in my stomach.

I know I can't blame myself for this. I don't even know if I can blame Travis. From what the nurse explained, sometimes there are just complications. But maybe if I'd been with her, if I hadn't left her alone, even for those few hours, maybe she wouldn't be in there right now fighting for her life.

I bury my face in my hands and choke back a sob.

The doors open, and a nurse runs out, down the hall.

I look up at the clock on the wall, each second stretching out as time moves excruciatingly slow.

Tick.

Tick.

Tick.

Each moment that passes, I prepare my heart for the worst. Bracing myself for the impact of losing the only woman I've ever loved.

Live, I pray silently. *Live, damn it.*

A deep, guttural sound fills the air, and it takes me a moment to realize that it's coming from me. I bury my face in my hands again and let grief wrack through me, because my strength is completely shattered.

"Sir?" A nurse crouches beside me.

I blink up at her, pleading with my eyes for good news, not ready for anything else.

"She's stable. You can see her now."

CHAPTER 28

LAYLA

*W*hen I try to open my eyes, it's like they're being weighed down by cement. Sluggishly, I blink them open. Fluorescent lights, and the sound of beeping, make me feel like I'm on a really bad techno acid trip. It takes me a moment to realize I'm in a hospital room.

The baby. Panic surges through me, causing the beeping to speed up. Frantic, my eyes dart around the room.

Carter is instantly beside me, taking my hand, and stroking my cheek. "Hey, it's okay. You're all right. I'm here."

"Carter." My voice feels like it's coated in asphalt.

"I'm here." There are dark circles under his eyes.

"The…baby."

"He's fine." He continues to stroke my cheek.

"He?"

Carter's lips twist up in a small smile, and when he starts to move away, I instantly panic.

"I'm not leaving." He kisses my forehead, then straightens.

I watch him move around my bed to a small bassinette that's positioned beside the chair he must have been sleeping in, evidenced by the pillow and blanket, and I wonder how long I've been out for.

Carefully, Carter reaches in and picks up the small bundle, eliciting a small cry.

"Your mommy wants to meet you," Carter whispers, cradling the small bundle against his chest like he's the most precious thing in the world.

I try to sit up, but I'm so weak I can barely shift myself even an inch.

Carter moves beside me, and he holds the baby so that I can see him.

He's beautiful. Tiny little nose, full bow lips that purse in his sleep. Instantly, my eyes cloud with tears.

"Hello, Joshua." I'm able to bring my hand up to gently stroke my fingers across his cheek. I want to hold him, but already the heaviness of sleep pulls at me, and I know I'm not strong enough.

"Joshua?" Carter says, smiling. "That was my father's name."

"I know." I try to smile back, but my face feels heavy, and despite my efforts to keep them open, my eyelids flutter closed. It takes all my strength to open them again. "What...happened?"

"You don't remember?" His brows draw down.

"Travis came back," I say, as images start to form a memory.

"Did he..." A muscle in Carter's jaw bunches. "I need to know if he hurt you."

"He didn't mean to." My words are slurred, each one an effort to say.

"Did he hit you?"

"No."

Carter breathes out a heavy breath and nods.

"I'm so tired."

"Rest." He presses his lips against my forehead.

"Don't leave." My eyes shut, and I feel myself being pulled back into the warmth of sleep.

"I won't leave either of you. I promise."

CHAPTER 29

CARTER

"*How* is she?" Travis hovers by the hospital room door, his grief-stricken gaze resting on Layla.

I grind my back teeth and take a steadying breath. The baby in my arms is the only thing stopping me from lashing out at my brother.

"You shouldn't be here."

"I know." He winces and looks down at the floor. "I just wanted to check on her. On..." His gaze drops to the bundle in my arms, and his eyes widen slightly. "He's...small."

"Babies are," I grunt, holding Joshua closer, every possessive instinct stirring inside me.

"I know. I've just never seen one so new." He rubs the back of his neck. "Did she name him?"

"Joshua."

"After Dad?" His brows draw up.

I nod.

"That's good. He would have liked that."

Layla stirs, but she doesn't wake.

"What did the police say?" I ask, watching him suspiciously. I hate that it's come to this between us, but I don't know how things will ever be different now.

Travis shifts from one foot to the other nervously.

"They took my statement. The paramedics called them when they saw my hand. They wanted to know if I...hit her. I'm not sure if they believed me. I think they're going to want to talk to Layla when she's awake."

"She told me that you didn't hit her."

Relief floods his face, like he wasn't sure what she'd say. "The police want me to stay in town for a couple days."

I narrow my gaze on him.

"Don't worry. I'll just go back to the house to get my stuff. I'll be gone before she's ready to go home."

I don't say anything, just watch him, feeling the chasm that's between us. Maybe it's always been there, or maybe I put it there. I just know that I barely know the man standing in front of me.

"You really do love her, don't you?" His brows are drawn down as he looks betweenher and I.

"More than anything," I say truthfully.

He exhales heavily. "That's good. I know they'll both be safe with you."

I give a brisk nod, still wary. "They're my family now. And I'll do anything to protect them."

"I know."

My throat clenches shut, and I force the next words out of my mouth. "But you're Joshua's biological father. If you want to be part of his life, I won't stop you."

Travis looks at me hard for a long moment, then he shakes his head. "Once I'm cleared, I'm going to head north again. For good. It's better that way. For everyone."

I can't say I'm not relieved by his decision, but my chest also hurts at what I'm losing. What I've already lost.

"You're still my brother, Travis. That won't change."

He leans against the wall, a sad smile playing on his lips. "For a long time, I blamed you for Dad. Felt like you took him away from me when you pulled the plug."

"I didn't have a choice." My defenses immediately go up.

"Yes, you did." He puts a hand up to stop me when I open my mouth to argue. "You could have waited until I'd gotten better. Given me a chance to say goodbye."

"He was already gone. He wouldn't have known you were there."

"But *I* would have known."

The truth hits me. I'd never really understood his anger until right now. Making the decision without him was only one in a long list of times when I'd treated him as something less – never an equal.

I lost more than just my parents that day. I also lost my brother.

"I'm sorry for not waiting, and for not being around more. Maybe things would have been different if I had."

"Maybe." He gives me one of his crooked grins, but there's only sad acceptance in his eyes. "But then, I've always been a screw-up."

I can't argue with that.

"You don't have to be."

He chuckles. "Yeah, but then where's the fun in that? Live fast, die hard, right?"

I shake my head at him. "You've got a second chance here. Don't fuck it up."

"Yeah." His lips tighten, then he glances once more at Joshua, his expression tightening. "He's going to be one lucky kid."

I frown, hearing the goodbye in his voice.

With a sigh, he turns and disappears out the door, and I know it's going to be a long time before I see or hear from him again.

CHAPTER 30

LAYLA

*M*y body is slowly healing. It's taken almost three months, but I'm starting to feel like myself again. Well, myself with a new appreciation of life and second chances.

Almost dying will do that to you.

Walking down the stairs doesn't hurt as much as it did, or take as much effort.

I can hear Carter in the living room, and Joshua's soft coos in response to whatever Carter is saying to him.

My mouth tugs up when I take the last step and see the two of them on the couch, Joshua in Carter's lap as he reads to him.

Joshua's eyes widen and he flaps his tiny fists excitedly when Carter flips the page.

I lean against the wall and watch them, my heart swelling.

This.

Carter.

Joshua.

My family.

It's more than I'd ever thought I'd get. More than I ever thought I deserved.

I never saw Travis after what happened. He sent me a letter a few weeks ago, apologizing and promising he'd stay out of our lives. That he'll never do anything to come between Carter and I.

In a way, I feel sorry for him. I know he lost in all this. Yes, he made some bad choices, but I hope one day that he and Carter will be able to reconcile.

I don't know what that'll look like, but I can't live in fear. Carter is Joshua's father now. Legally and emotionally.

He's done everything for both of us during my recovery. Sometimes, I'm awed by how easy he fell into the role. I'm still struggling a bit, but each day it gets better, and with Carter's support, I'm learning.

My chest squeezes with how much I love him. Both of them.

Joshua lets out a small squeal of delight, and Carter laughs with him.

Every time I see them together, my heart does this little dance in my chest. Seeing the mountain of a man, with his dark ink and rough callused hands, being so gentle, makes me fall in love with him all over again. And I didn't think I could love him any more than I already did.

The epitome of everything my mother ever warned me about. I chuckle under my breath, because right from the start he'd been my hero. I just couldn't see it.

As if sensing my presence, Carter glances over at me and smiles. "Hi."

"Hi." I grin back, my skin warming just from a single look. "It's his naptime."

"Awe, Mom," Carter teases. "Just one more book."

I laugh and nod, watching him pick up another little cardboard book and start his exaggerated rendition of the ABCs.

For so long, I'd tried to fight my feelings for him, fear motivating my every action. Always afraid that if I let myself believe in something good, that it would be ripped away from me. I'm not saying that it isn't always a possibility. Life is chaos, and sometimes brutal. But hiding from happiness only guarantees you'll never get it. It's better to experience each moment fully, than to spend your whole life isolated and alone.

"Marry me," I say, making Carter's gaze jerk back to mine. I lick my lips, and repeat, "Marry me."

His expression is serious, but he doesn't say anything. He just stands and places Joshua in the playpen, then he turns back to me.

"Ask me again," he demands, stalking towards me with heat in his gaze.

I grin up at him and tease, "I'm only asking once. If that's not good enough–"

His lips crash down on mine.

"Yes," he growls against my mouth, kissing me harder.

I wrap my arms around his neck and give into the heat and possessiveness of the kiss.

His fingers tangle in my hair, and when he pulls back, I can see the elation in his eyes. No man has or will ever make me feel the way he does with one single glance. Like I'm important and cherished.

I glance over at Joshua through the mesh of the playpen. It's past his naptime, and already his eyes are closing. "Looks like we have at least thirty minutes to ourselves."

Carter gives me a wicked grin, the one that after all this time still gives me butterflies. The next thing I know, he's lifting me against his chest and carrying me upstairs to the bedroom, his hands moving over my body to get rid of my clothing.

When we're both naked, he brings his hands to my waist and places a hard kiss on my mouth.

"I love you," I say, running my fingers across the new ink on his chest. Mine and Joshua's name are written in a beautiful design over his heart.

His hands cup my face, drawing my gaze up to his eyes.

Blue.

Intense.

Captivating.

And so full of love that my breath gets locked somewhere in the back of my throat.

Every sculpted inch of his body radiates strength and possessiveness. There's no fear when I'm with him because I've finally given myself to him, completely.

EPILOGUE

CARTER

Three years later...

I can feel Layla's eyes on me with every flip of the page. It's her manuscript, the second draft of the one she originally wrote, and it's good. Really good. Not only because it's well written, but because, in a way, it's our story.

Two people who have to face seemingly insurmountable obstacles to be together.

I read the final paragraph and my chest squeezes, because she's written her happy ending. No, *our* happy ending.

She knew that no matter how much they had lost, they had gained so much more. He was her one. The one. The only person who had ever made her feel truly and completely loved. It didn't matter what the world thought of them, because with him by her side, every day was a fairytale come to life. And he was her happily ever after.

"WELL?" she asks when I place the papers on the table beside the bed. "What do you think?"

"It's good."

"Really?"

"Really." I grab her around the waist and pull her down on my lap. "I'm proud of you."

She gives me a small smile. "I'd never have finished it without you."

"See. All my prodding worked."

"Maybe. But that's not what I meant. I would never have believed in the ending if I hadn't met you. You're the one that showed me happiness is possible." Her brows draw down, and she says softly, "Even through heartbreak."

I press my lips against her forehead, and let her words sink in.

Both of our lives have been filled with tragedy, and these past three years haven't been any different.

Six months ago, I received a phone call informing me that Travis had been killed in a boating accident. He'd been drinking with a few of his buddies up on Lake Ontario. From what I was told, he'd been sitting on the side of the boat when he'd gone overboard, hitting his head when he fell. They pulled his body out three days later.

I swallow past the large lump that forms in my throat.

There will always be a part of me that feels guilty for not being more for him. But Travis made his own choices. Choices that almost always went against every piece of advice I'd given him.

We'd spoken a few times before his accident. And I'd sent him a couple pictures of Joshua.

I'd thought he'd gotten his head straightened out. Or, at

least, that's what it seemed. He was always good at pretending with me.

Hit with a wave of sorrow, my chest clenches painfully.

"You're thinking about him?" Layla straddles me and places her palms on my cheeks.

I give a small nod, my throat tightening with the memories.

"I'm sorry," she says, her brown eyes filled with sympathy and regret.

Pressing my forehead against hers, I inhale her scent, focusing on the good that's in front of me.

And it is good.

My life is everything I never knew I wanted.

Husband.

Father.

Those two things have completed me, made me whole.

I kiss her hard, needing her touch. I'm always amazed at how we can both draw strength from each other with the simplest of gestures.

"Have you thought of a title yet?" I ask, going back to the manuscript she's been working so hard on.

"I was thinking about Second Draft." Her hands comb through my hair, a small smile playing on her lips. "The book is all about second chances, rewriting mistakes, and turning them into something positive and beautiful, even if the world doesn't understand it."

"Like us." I trace my thumb over her bottom lip.

"Like us," she agrees.

We're bound in a way that defies even my own understanding. Every pain, every happiness we experience, we experience together. Maybe it's all the things we've already been through together, or maybe there really is something in the whole soulmate claim.

I don't know. What I do know is that my heart and soul

are tangled with hers. And there isn't a day that goes by that I don't send up a prayer of thanks that she wasn't taken from me the day Joshua was born.

"Joshua's sleeping," she whispers, fingers curling under my shirt, and my cock is instantly hard the minute her hands brush against my lower abs.

"And?" I ask, knowing full well her meaning.

Her fingertips skim up my chest, tugging the t-shirt over my head. "*And* I want my husband to make love to me."

I flip her on her back and she lets out a small squeal. "After those steamy scenes you made me read, I was hoping you were going to say that."

She chuckles lightly, helping me remove her shirt, then wiggles out of her pants.

I have my own pants off in seconds, the need to be inside of her overwhelming. Her hands begin their frantic dance across my chest, down my hips, wrapping around the length of my cock and guiding it towards her entrance.

"Patience, sweetheart." I growl against her lips, reaching between her legs to make sure she's ready for me, which she is. I sink one finger into her wet folds, circling her clit until she's mewling in pleasure.

"Carter," she moans, gripping my hips and squirming beneath me, begging me for my cock within her body.

A wild cry falls from her lips as I sink into her.

Feeling her slick heat wrapped tight around me is like being immersed in a vortex of all consuming rapture. There's no better feeling in the world. Not when those light brown eyes stare up at me with more love than any man could ever deserve.

I draw back, then thrust hard, making her cry out again.

My movements are slow and controlled, needing to keep my head, long enough to make her come before spilling myself inside of her.

The noises she makes as her body begins the climb towards her climax nearly undo me, and I crash my lips against hers, thrusting harder and faster, kissing her like a man starved. She strains against me, her legs tightening around my hips.

Heavy lidded and face flushed, her head tilts back. Her body spasms around me, milking my cock and triggering my own release, until I'm spurting hard and deep inside her.

I gather her close and roll onto my side, bringing her with me, burying my lips against her hair.

"I love you so fucking much it hurts, baby."

"I know," she says, still breathing hard, and grinning up at me.

And she does, which in its own right is a miracle.

"I love you, too." Her hands are on my chest, eyes alight with something I can't decipher.

I drag my thumb across the line of her jaw. So fucking beautiful. There are some days when I still can't believe how lucky I am.

Today is one of them.

She chews on her lip, tracing the patterns on my chest, one finger copying the letters of her and Joshua's names that are printed over my heart.

"What are you thinking?"

"I was just wondering how you're going to fit another name here."

My brows draw down until I realize what she's saying. We've been trying to have another baby for over a year now with no luck, and I'm almost afraid to ask. "Are you..."

"Yes." The smile that lightens her face makes my chest tighten.

I plant a hard kiss on her lips, cupping her jaw in my hands.

"Are you happy?" she asks.

"God, yes." I kiss her again, blinking back the tears that prick my eyes. Being a father is the second best thing in my life, the first being her husband.

"Daddy, Daddy." There's a rush of tiny footsteps clambering down the hall towards our room, causing both Layla and I to reach for our clothes.

I barely finish shoving my legs into my pants when Joshua's tear-streaked face appears at our door. I scoop him up, and immediately his arms wrap tight around my neck.

"Monster in my closet," he says, tightening his grip.

"There are no monsters, buddy," I say, tickling him until his tears turn to full-out belly laughs.

"I wanna sleep with you and Mommy."

"Big boys sleep in their own beds," Layla says sternly.

"Daddy sleeps in your bed."

I chuckle, despite the look of warning Layla gives me. "That's 'cause I'm married to Mommy."

"Please," he begs.

I grunt and glance over at Layla, who's already sighing with resignation because we both know that if we don't let him, he'll be crawling back into bed with us every twenty minutes.

"Give your mom a hug," I say, putting him on the bed and watching him scamper across and jump into Layla's arms.

"Right to sleep," she warns, brushing his light brown hair off his forehead.

I crawl in beside them and smile, despite knowing I'm probably not going to sleep much tonight. The kid is as active in his sleep as he is awake.

As soon as I lie down, Joshua jumps on my chest, making my breath leave me in a whoosh. "Careful."

"Story," he pleads. His brown eyes, the same color as Layla's, are wide awake now.

Layla just smiles and gives me that I-told-you-so look.

"One short story," I say.

"About hockey." His grin gets bigger.

The kid loves the game already. I bought him his first set of skates this past winter, and next year I've decided to coach the Little Tykes program.

"I've got a better story," I say, tapping his nose gently. "About a little boy who's going to be a big brother."

Joshua frowns. "No. Hockey story."

Layla chuckles and shakes her head.

"What? Babies aren't as fun as hockey?" I grin.

"No." He shakes his head, brows drawn down.

Laughing, I muss his hair. "There was a time I would have agreed with you, buddy."

His nose scrunches up.

"But now?" Layla asks, one eyebrow raised, a grin playing on her lips.

I place my hand on her stomach and smile. "Now, there's nothing that makes me happier."

ABOUT THE AUTHOR

Amazon bestselling author C.M. Seabrook writes hot, steamy romances with possessive bad boys, and the passionate, fiery women who love them.

Swoonworthy romances from the heart!

When she isn't reading or writing sexy stories, she's most likely spending time with her family, cooking, singing, or racing between soccer, hockey and karate practices. She's living her own happily ever after with her husband of fifteen years and their two daughters.

www.cmseabrook.com
chantelseabrook@gmail.com